To my very
Gasam
From Dirty Dai

25 April 2009

CW01430483

Poor Little Chess Boy

Dai Llewellyn

authorHOUSE®

AuthorHouse™ UK Ltd.
500 Avebury Boulevard
Central Milton Keynes, MK9 2BE
www.authorhouse.co.uk
Phone: 08001974150

First published by AuthorHouse 2/11/2009

ISBN: 978-1-4389-5756-2

Printed in the United States of America
Bloomington, Indiana

This book is printed on acid-free paper.

To my wife and children

'The Queen of Hearts, she made some tarts,

All on a summer day:

The Knave of Hearts, he stole those tarts

And took them quite away':

Alice in Wonderland by Lewis Carroll

INTRODUCTION

Most of what I have written is true. Some of it isn't. I leave it to you, the reader, to decide which is which. I have to say that I am not sure myself, so the task is all the more difficult for you to discern.

What I can say with more certainty is that the bits that straddle the line between fact and fiction do not detract from the impact of the story or the overall integrity of its content.

Given the passage of time – and this book covers a period of nearly 50 years – one's memory can be forgiven for playing tricks. However, I am confident that I have not knowingly misrepresented the essence of that which unfolds before your very eyes. Those individuals whose roles are more controversial, not to say vulnerable, have had their identities protected.

I am extremely lucky to have led such a diverse and interesting life, which I have largely forged myself, but in the process I have been given a lot of nudges forward by too many people to record. I would, however, give a special mention to the last real head of the Immigration Service, one Peter Tompkins, who gave me the biggest shove forward, for which I shall be forever grateful.

The world of espionage is a murky one indeed, and not lightly entered into. By contrast, the world of subject-specific intelligence, of pioneering enforcement work and of challenging overseas projects and postings are hugely satisfying. Let the action begin, albeit slowly.................

CHAPTER 1

Life was good. After 5 years of turgid, tediously boring employment as an insignificant, low-paid and junior civil servant in two government departments, I, Dai Morgan found myself as a newly appointed immigration officer at London's second airport – Gatwick, also unkindly referred to at the time as France's second cigarette. The month was December and the year was 1970, when Gatwick had a single terminal (as it still does) and was seen as the poor relation to the burgeoning Heathrow airport, known to those who worked there as Hedgerow and later as Thiefrow, allegedly because some of the (then) baggage handlers' propensity to steal from outgoing and incoming luggage. Now they just lose them! Anyway, I digress.

Just 3 weeks earlier, I had married my long-time girlfriend, Rhiannon at a quickly arranged ceremony in our hometown Register Office. The good folk in our part of Cardiff had assumed that this was predicated on yet another South Walean pre-marital pregnancy – then not uncommon, now all too frequent – a supposition underpinned by the fact the couple was moving away. Not just out of South Wales, but to England; and not just to England, but to one of its eastern-most counties. It might just as well have been Siberia as far as they were concerned. 'A sure sign of guilt, Boyo', was a common refrain at the time.

What the locals hadn't realised was that the British civil service financially rewards its married transferees far more than its single ones. Not that reward was uppermost in my thoughts. Rhiannon and I had been together for over 4 years and would have spliced the knot sooner or later (probably). I was 24 and she was 21. The respective families, once satisfied that the hastily arranged marriage was taking place for all the right reasons, were more than happy to give it their blessing, not least because the cost of a Register Office wedding was considerably lower than a church or chapel one. Money was tight and, after all, the longevity of the union far outweighed the initial means of achieving it.

The reception was equally low-key. Just 14 guests, including Rhiannon and me, took place at a local hotel, which provided a decent lunch and a convivial atmosphere. The speech by my best man, Marcus, was suitably rude and, in parts, very rude, but a good time was had by all with none of the drawbacks of an expensive, showcase wedding.

The honeymoon was similarly planned on pragmatic rather than romantic grounds. It began with two nights at an AA recommended manor house in mid-Sussex occupied almost entirely by resident geriatrics, who viewed the young couple with some amusement, not to say curiosity. We were the youngest incumbents by several decades and initially felt we were staying in an expensive nursing home. On returning to the hotel on the first night after a couple of drinks at a nearby pub (and not yet 10.30pm), we found ourselves locked out without a key. Thankfully, the in-house doyen of the premises, a Major something-or-other, smelling strongly of cognac of cognac and pipe tobacco, was still engaged in an illicit card game with his cronies, gallantly came to our rescue.

"This is not good enough!", he thundered. "What is the world coming to when two newly weds are denied their conjugal rights because the governor wants an early night? Come in, sit down and have a drink on me!"

The following day, there were abject apologies from the management, but only a freebee half bottle of cheap champagne to mark their remorse.

Moving on, but not very far, we found ourselves in sunny Brighton – quite something considering it was December – albeit in a much-reduced standard of accommodation. The emphasis now was to find somewhere for me to stay when I took up post at Gatwick airport some 2 weeks' hence. That said, we enjoyed a modicum of interesting sightseeing and, it has to be said an abject and long-lasting disappointment, on Rhiannon's part, from anything resembling a proper, planned honeymoon. Hey ho, things could only get worse.

CHAPTER 2

Before you fall off your perch with boredom, hang on in there – it gets a lot more interesting, not to say dramatic as, the story unfolds. You'll miss a truly great yarn if you don't. Don't say I didn't warn you.

I subsequently took up post at Gatwick shortly before Christmas 1970 and was joined by Rhiannon a month or so later. We were allocated a council flat in nearby Horley, before moving into our first owned accommodation, which was a very nice semi-detached Sussex bungalow (costing the princely sum of £6,600) in Hayward's Heath, just a few miles north of Brighton. This was a time of gazumping, when prices were rising at an alarming pace and when many house sellers did not flinch from accepting higher offers even after accepting an earlier one.

The lead-in to all of this provides an insight into to what was to follow. Although not an academic by nature, I had been something of a child chess prodigy. I was fortunate to have had a gifted History teacher, one Derek Powell, who was an Oxbridge graduate and a keen, if somewhat limited, chess player, who made the school team one of the best in the United Kingdom. Rather than concentrate on my GCE 'O' Level lessons, I and my partner-in-crime, John Woodcutt preferred to play mental chess and would often get to move 30+ before the inevitable teacher's board rubber came flying past our ears. To everyone's surprise, I went on to win the Welsh under 13 championship, following which, and at the same age, was selected for the senior county and junior (under 18) national teams, which I represented for 3 years. One of my all time achievements was when I played against Grand Master Paul Keres, the Estonian who was rightly hailed as the best chess player never to have won the World crown, despite having nearly done so on no less than 5 occasions. As with so many talented people, WW2 intervened at the peak of his powers and he, like Jimmy White much later in the snooker arena, but for different reasons, was destined not to achieve the highest accolade. Paul Keres was on a European tour and had agreed to play a simultaneous chess match against 30 young Cardiff aspirants. I was the only opponent to beat him and was immensely proud when Mr Keres shook my hand and said: "Well done, you played very well for one so young." I then came very close to winning the British Junior championship, which I had agonisingly led for most of the rounds, failing only at the last hurdle to two lesser opponents. This had a lasting affect because I knew I had bottled it. As a result, I vowed never to play competitive chess again. My ability and achievements, however, had not been lost on a certain arm of the British security services, a serving member of which approached me in the early part of 1964, posing initially as a careers officer for the Civil Service, for which I had just been accepted, but subsequently introduced himself as a serving member the Secret Intelligence Service (SIS), also known as MI6. The *imprimatur*, however, was that I should reveal this meeting to no-one ('and I mean **NO-ONE** boy!').

I was left with the distinct impression that something 'unusual' would happen 'at some time in the future' once I had become a government officer, which I duly did in May 1964. I found myself working for the Ministry of Transport (MOT) under the management of the diminutive Ernest Marples, whom, curiously, I met for the first and only time in the his private lift at St Christopher House, Southwick Street, London SE1. The

Secretary of State's minders had tried to evict me, but Ernest wasn't having any of it and insisted 'the young man remain where he was until he reached his floor.'

My brief time in the MOT was not a particularly happy one, and within 18 months, I transferred to the London Passport Office in Petty France, SW1 with the intention of moving to Newport when the new office opened there in 1967. A year earlier (1966 and all that) I had started going out with Rhiannon, which was the main reason for my return to what Dylan Thomas aptly described as ' the land of my fathers and my fathers are welcome to it'.

I did not dwell on my secret meeting, which I did not fully understand and which I did not think would amount to anything. To my immense surprise, a second approach was made in 1965 when I was on day release from the Ministry of Transport studying A Level economics at the London School of Economics. Sat alone at a table in the school's canteen, I was surprised to see the same secret squirrel quietly, almost invisibly, joining me with a benign look on his face and clearly a message to impart. The conversation, as with the last meeting, was one-sided and equally enigmatic.

"Dear boy, what a fortuitous coincidence that we find one another in the same place at the same time. How the devil are you? And how is that chess game of yours going?"

I was completely nonplussed and could manage only a gulp and a blank stare. The man looked like a university professor, both urbane and wise, and had a glint in his eye suggesting that he saw, heard and spoke no evil. He formally introduced himself as an SIS recruitment officer and went on to explain that his 'masters' wanted him to recruit me in an informal and as yet undefined role because it was felt I might (just might) usefully contribute to the national good at some time in the future. No promises though and, in fact, the relationship would in all probability amount to nothing.

"And how, young Sir, do you think you might respond to such an offer?".

How indeed? I was not happy with my current lot and replied more in hope than expectation.

"What can an insignificant junior civil servant do for the national good? OK I used to play good chess, but not that good and I have nothing else going for me that makes me special."

Hayden smiled knowingly and replied that his service believed there was a potential to be fulfilled, but that potential was an ephemeral quality, which could lead to great things or wither on the vine. And usually did.

At that point I was joined by an LSE friend called Mona, who sat down at the same time that Hayden spirited himself away as if he were never there. "Who was that?" came the question.

"Just one of the lecturers who thinks I have the potential to become a future Chancellor of the Exchequer", I replied.

The deed, apparently, was done.

CHAPTER 3

Life shortly thereafter was bit of a blur. I pursued a position of survival rather than personal advancement and nothing of particular note interrupted my day-to-day oxygen intake. Rather, the keynotes were boredom, lack of money and a growing sense of personal failure.

I was never one to feel confident in my ability to take on the world. On the contrary, I worried about my physical under-development, which manifested itself in various ways. At the age of 18 I looked 14 or 15, which meant that I was regularly and embarrassingly refused drinks in pubs; that I was not always taken seriously by my peers; and that I avoided situations that could possibly lead to loss of face. For most of the time I spent in London between 1964 and 1967 I was a total and utter emotional mess, bordering on mental breakdown.

An example of my lack of maturity was my first shave, which took place in the London hostel I occupied in South Kensington. The removal of my down-like hair almost resulted in the need for a blood transfusion. Unusually, I was alone in the room I shared with three other young Civil Servants. A newly bought shaver and shaving soap rested on the washbasin looking at me somewhat threateningly. Within minutes of starting the shaving process my face was covered in blood, which took a long time to staunch, and my self-confidence took yet another knock at a time when I really needed some tender loving care. It took 3 days for the wounds to heal, and, to the credit of my room mates, no-one said a word.

Money though was very tight and, like most of my 1964/65 contemporaries, I was forced to take a second job. This turned out to be a washer-upperer in the posh Kenco Coffee House in Knightsbridge, where patrons paid as much as two shillings and sixpence for a pastry and coffee. The upshot was that I got back to the hostel from the MOT at around 5.30pm, ate a hurried dinner and was hard at work from 6.30pm until midnight 5 nights a week. Working a 70 hour week, I earned the princely sum of £50 a month. Ronaldo and co, eat your hearts out!

One of my abiding memories was the sight of the Nigerian pastry chef in the almost unbearable heat of the basement kitchen dripping sweat from his chin into the very pastries that the Grande Dames of London were paying a small fortune for. I earned enough money to pay, more or less, for my daily outgoings and for a cheap set of golf clubs purchased at a knock-down price. This was to become my pride and joy and also a means of making useful contacts in the MOT and beyond.

The upshot of this enervating moonlighting did nothing for my advancement within the Civil Service. Quite the contrary, I was always lacking in energy and vitality, was transferred to another section within the Highways, Land and Legal section of the MOT as an under-achiever, but regrettably all to no avail. That said, I made some good friends along the way and successfully represented the department at a decent level in table tennis. I thought of joining the departmental chess club, attended only one club night, beat the MOT champion without breaking stride and never went there again. The memories remained painful.

Despite these set backs, I was a resilient bugger with a big heart and a will to win to an almost fanatical level. I had failed in the biggest contest of my (chess) life and had vowed never to capitulate again to inferior opposition.

Before moving out of the South Kensington hostel, I experienced the immense pleasure of peeing out of my third floor bedroom window onto a pink van that had been parked outside the building for some time. This was after a boatload of beer and because the nearest toilet was two floors away. The sight of a head coming out of the sunroof looking up to the sky and wondering if it was raining was a bonus. Little did I know at the time that I had just pissed on the emerging Pink Floyd band, whose name was emblazoned on the side of the van!

Moving on and somewhat reluctantly, I accepted an invitation to stay in Battersea, SW11 with an older colleague from the Ministry of Transport, a decision that would have yet another negative affect on my mental stability.

Gerald was a very good friend and a talented artist. His problem was that he was infatuated with me and, despite his huge generosity, he was jealous of anyone, male or female, whom he considered to be a rival.

An example of this was when I decided to lose my virginity. The build up to this momentous event was comical on the scale of a Brian Rix farce. Robby was another MOT colleague, who had the 'hots' for me and who was not shy showing it. For some months the relationship was non-existent, just merely hinted at. We were of a similar age, both lacking in experience and confidence, and looking for something neither of us knew or could fully comprehend.

The hormones were rising, so much so that I decided to take a leap in the dark and invite Robby over to Battersea for a flirtatious evening (meaning I badly wanted a shag). At first Robby was not keen to accept the invitation, only because she knew it was not the best time for her. My perseverance won her over and we duly met in a Battersea pub for a drink and a chat. One thing led to another and we moved from the pub to my shared flat. I had asked Gerald to make himself scarce, which he reluctantly did.

The bedroom scene led to a fumbling grope in the dark, followed by a desperate attempt to place my rampant penis in a place I had heard about, but had only a rough anatomical idea of the where to aim. I soon learned that Robby's earlier reluctance was predicated on the problems associated with the menstrual cycle and the enormous padding that accompanied it in those days. The penetration was not easy or particularly pleasurable, and certainly not helped by the sound of the locked bedroom door being ripped off its hinges by a very drunk Gerald intent on finding out what his 'Boy' was up to. Robby reacted like a startled rabbit exactly at the time that I decide to move into climactic overdrive. Not only did the earth move, but the room did as well as Gerald propelled himself from door to floor in one slow but very loud movement. God, I thought, you couldn't make it up.

A difficult moment for all concerned. Fortunately Gerald did not stir from his prostrate position for some time, long enough for us to get dressed and leave the premises with what can only be described as mixed feelings. We walked to the nearest bus stop, spoke awkwardly until the red chariot arrived and, embarrassment on both sides, never saw one another again.

Hot on the heels of this momentous event, I found myself on an LSE sponsored visit to a cigarette factory in West London with the aim of putting the Law of Diminishing Returns to the test in a real-life situation. This economic law, developed and promoted by Thomas Malthus and others, can be applied to a variety of work and leisure situations. Basically, it proclaims that, beyond some point, each additional unit of variable input yields less and less additional output. This can be anything from 'the first fag of the day is better than the next and so on', to 'a factory's production pro rata efficiency decreases with increased investment'. Mona and I found ourselves otherwise alone in the bowels of the factory with no clear view of what we were supposed to be doing. The noise of the turbines made communication very difficult, so much so that we had to shout into one another's ear to make ourselves heard.

It was in this close-encounter situation that Mona took hold of my right hand and guided it between her legs making me acutely aware that she was not wearing knickers under her leather mini skirt. I looked at her questioningly and saw a wicked glint in her eye.

"Good God", I thought, "nearly 19 years of virginity and, within a week, I've got pussy galore!"

It took but a moment for me to pull out my proud 'old man' and place it exactly where Mona wanted it, causing her, unnervingly, to burst into operatic song (I knew she was mainly a music student and later discovered that she was a Wagner fan and was currently auditioning for the part of Freia, the goddess of youth and beauty, in a student production of Das Rheingold). Her voice carried the competing roar of the factory turbines and she managed to hit high C just as I reached my own, less cerebral climax, the whole business having been concluded in less than 3 minutes.

Whilst adjusting my dress, I smilingly said to Mona: "I don't think that this was how our tutor expected us to test our understanding of the Law of Diminishing Returns, do you?"

She replied by saying: "Was that only the first of the day for you?" We both fell about laughing.

The moment was but a brief and pleasant interlude in what was otherwise an unhappy time of my life. Time, however, moved on and my thoughts projected to an existence beyond the Great Wen, of which I had had more than my fill. I was on the verge of a mental breakdown, the causal effects of which were complex and disturbing. Depression has been described as the lie detector of last resort, and I showed many of the symptoms.

CHAPTER 4

I knew I needed something that was missing in my life, but did not know what that was or how I would find it.

Enter Rhiannon, who would prove to be my saviour and the love of my life. We had first met when I was seventeen and she fourteen. This was at a local church get-together in Cardiff, which featured some basic popular music, no alcohol or anything else the Boys' Brigade or Girls' Guide would have disapproved of. The night was the very personification of innocence, with a slight undercurrent of 'who fancied whom' and would this lead to a snog with tongues but no touching of private parts? In fact, our only contact was when she hit me on the head with a rolled up newspaper. Well, you have to start somewhere.

There was no further contact until 1966, though I (and possibly Rhiannon) felt there was a possibility we might eventually move to another level of compatibility. She, at the time, was courting the son of the Manse, who was one of my old school friends and who fancied himself (somewhat comically) as a Jack the Lad. He had turned his attentions to another young lady, who also had well-developed breasts, but who was very much what the youth of today refer to as a chav. Not a relationship to last the test of time, but hopefully he and she happily coincided for a while. He was certainly not a happy chappy when he found out that I had stolen Rhiannon from under his nose, the result of which was a total breakdown in communication forever and a day. No great loss there then.

I was not slow to develop a relationship with Rhiannon, and, following a few nervous meetings with her and her family and my reluctant return to London, we commenced a yearlong period of intensive correspondence. What had not been said face-to-face was more than compensated for by means of the written word and a growing feeling that we were meant for one another. Romantic, eh?

When the South Wales Passport Office opened in 1967, I found myself on a train travelling from Paddington to my near hometown and salvation.

The journey, though, was quite eventful. Enter one Jonny 'the Boyo' Phillips, who had also transferred to the new Welsh Passport Office. Jonny was from Barry, was an accomplished rugby player and long distance runner and, despite his slight frame, boasted a Hampton to be proud of (pun definitely intended).

Despite his other attributes, Jonny had a low boredom threshold and decided the best way to enjoy the train journey to Cardiff was to set light to my outspread Daily Telegraph. The result led to general mayhem within the carriage and a great deal of satisfaction by the perpetrator. Perhaps I had asked for my bubble to be pricked, and who better to do it than my mate Jonny. We enjoyed many more mutual experiences over the next 30+ years and never failed to acknowledge one another's talents. But that's another story.

Suffice to say at this moment in time that I was 'goin ome' and still not quite old enough to vote, not that the plebiscite was uppermost in my mind. I was young, relieved to be free of the stresses of London and looking forward to happier times. The next 3 years were to prove most interesting and hugely stimulating.

I returned briefly to the family home, but only long enough to remember how much I had hated it and for my mam and dad to decide I was no longer welcome, mainly my mam I have to say. This was more to do with my reluctance to be there than my parents' wish to see the back of me. If not already apparent, I was a wilful child who grew up to be a wilful young man and who, along the way, acquired the ability to manipulate those closest to me. This was not a talent I was particularly proud of. Quite the contrary, I despised this propensity to be a control freak, but, alas, never quite managed to rid myself of the tendency. I knew the writing was on the wall, or, more specifically when I found my golf clubs propped up against the (outside) of the front door with a note saying I should take them and my other belongings to another place and not return any time soon. Being the artful dodger, I had anticipated this scenario and had made plans to relocate with my mate Marcus (my best man to be), who was also experiencing accommodation problems. We found a house to rent, but needed two more tenants to cover the costs. The choice was limited and boiled down to a couple of fellows from Marcus' girlfriend's Department, both of whom hailed from west Wales and worked in the same building in which the Passport Office was located in Newport, some 10 miles east of Cardiff. The subsequent relationship turned out to be both challenging, read difficult, and entirely entertaining.

Our two housemates could not have been more disparate in character and personality. One was tall, boastful and strong willed, bordering on the insane; the other was a total wimp with aspirations to get through life with the minimum of dress sense, aggravation or fuss. By contrast, Marcus and I were very comfortable in one another's company and lost no opportunity to strengthen our relationship, even if this worked to the detriment of the other two, whose names are irrelevant for the purposes of this tome.

An example of our team work was when the west Waleans returned home one evening, in a state of some agitation, from a meeting at the local Civil Service club. There followed a heated argument about why the larger of the two, who was the treasurer of the club, had misappropriated a considerable amount of the club's funds. Retaliation was swift and wholly predictable.

Prior to their arrival, we had secreted ourselves in the loft, the hatch to which was immediately above the landing leading to the house's 3 bedrooms. Following the argument and the thuggish retribution visited upon the wimp, Marcus and I realised that the 2 house-mates had taken to their respective, adjacent bedrooms. Out came the old rugby boot on a piece of string, which was used to bang on both bedroom doors in the certain knowledge that their targets would react in exactly the way they did, the hatch being closed just before either could identify the source.

"What the fuck are you doing?", came the question from Large to Little. "Nothing you cheating bastard", came the retort. Silence for a few minutes. Then the boot struck again, only louder and more menacingly. "Right, that's it, I'm going to kill you, you bastard", announced Large. "Go on then you embezzling twat, see if I care". Doors opened and were slammed shut, another squeal of pain was heard from Little, then again total silence. It was all we could do to stifle our amusement, not least because we feared that Large's response, were he to discover our presence and involvement, would have caused us much, much pain.

In the event, Large was the one to take fright, to the point that he was discovered the next morning on the couch in the living room fast asleep with a kitchen knife on his chest. What joy this sight brought to us.

Not long after this episode, the foursome became a threesome. Exit west Wales, enter Yorkshire in the form of a very affable fellow, who fairly soon found himself a Welsh, tennis-playing wife-to-be and who also flew the nest. In fact, he was rarely off it as far as Dai and Marcus could hear from his adjoining bedroom. God, were they noisy.

Our tenancy agreement having expired, we found a one-bedroom flat in a nearby house owned and occupied by an accommodating couple. In fact, the wife was so accommodating that Marcus took full advantage and laid bare his full talents and a bit more besides. At least the rent did not go up whilst we were there.

From then on, our relationship went from strength to strength and verged upon, but did not quite match the outrageous escapades malignly captured in the film Clockwork Orange. We worked as a team and trusted one another implicitly. It was almost a marriage in the sense that we shared the same bedroom, loved listening to Led Zeppelin played very loudly late into the night and discussed topics of mutual interest.

One caper we came up with was to drive around selected low-life areas of Newport with a squeezy bottle filled with piss. We would stop to politely ask directions from someone we considered to be fair game, and, before the inevitable vitriol ensued, whoever was in the passenger seat would empty the contents of the bottle into the victim's face and the driver would gun the car out of sight, hopefully without stalling, the consequences of which were too horrible to contemplate. There was no rational reason for this childish behaviour, but, though completely immature, it provided us with a great deal of pleasure.

Another death-wish, daring-do, totally irresponsible act of madness was to drive Marcus' fast car down a steep, narrow road leading to one of Newport's hospitals at around 80 miles an hour in the certain knowledge that anything coming the other way would result in a head-on collision and death for all concerned. How so unforgivingly stupid, but how so stimulatingly gratifying. The adrenalin buzz remains unsurpassed.

We enjoyed all sorts of shared experiences, many of which could fill the pages of yet another book. Suffice to say that it was a happy time that would reach a sort of denouement when we both got married to our respective girlfriends.

CHAPTER 5

So, the story now returns to 1971, when Rhiannon and I were as one and living together on the Surrey/Sussex border close to Gatwick Airport. As has been related already, we moved from our temporary accommodation in Horley to a very nice, semi-detached bungalow in Burgess Hill, not far from Brighton – almost a full circle from our honeymoon the previous year.

I was on a career ladder which would lead to events far beyond my expectations and which would be the cause of a great deal of pleasure and pain, though not necessarily in that order.

In the short term, I learned to become a proficient immigration officer, largely but not wholly in good company, and possessed the happy and enduring knack of being able to make my own luck. My bosses at Gatwick airport were mostly supportive (it goes without saying that every organisation has its arseholes and Gatwick was no exception), and one of the good ones took a shine to the young Welshman, who was soon to test and stretch his boss' confidence in him. Graham was a Scottish chief immigration officer (CIO), who was a frequent visitor to the airside bar between flights, purely, of course, for surveillance purposes. On one occasion, Graham weaved his way from a pre-lunch drink at the upstairs bar to the Arrivals hall only to find it throbbing with queues of passengers. At that time, the French (and everyone else in the current EU) were subject to immigration control. Graham spotted a very attractive French lady standing in front of my desk, made his way to the point of examination and put his elbow on the raised top of the desk, unfortunately missing at the first attempt and found his chin very close to the passenger's ample breasts.

He quickly recovered his composure and, (wrongly) assuming the young lady did not speak a word of English, proceeded to deliver a most incisive summation of the situation as he saw it.

"Dai, I think you've got a real goer here; lovely arse I have to say". Having delivered these words of infinite wisdom, Graham resumed his upright stance and slowly aimed himself towards his office.

The lady in question turned out to be a university lecturer at the Sorbonne, who spoke immaculate English and who, not surprisingly, asked, nay demanded the name and position of that 'extremely rude man'.

Thinking on my feet, I apologised for the gross behaviour of a drunken person I had never seen before and whose identity was a complete mystery to me. But, rest assured, I would leave no stone unturned in bringing the miscreant to justice. Lies, it seemed, came easily to me.

Not long after, I found myself interviewing another attractive young lady, this time from Guyana. She had a student entry certificate in her passport and said she would be studying hairdressing at a well-known London college, for which purpose she held sufficient funds. On further examination, I elicited that the passenger's real intention was to remain permanently in the UK, a fact she had not divulged to the visa officer. At that time, the Immigration Rules applying to Commonwealth citizens were less than helpful, given there was no specific requirement for the applicant to intend to return to his or her home country at the end of the course.

I considered this to be a legal omission of some magnitude and proceeded to refer the case to the duty chief immigration officer for refusal of leave to enter on the ground that the passenger's **primary purpose** was to secure permanent residence, for which she required but did not hold an entirely different entry clearance. Having been rebuffed by the first CIO (read 'arsehole'), I approached a second one, who also told me I was wasting my time because the entry clearance could only be set aside if the applicant had made a false statement to obtain it, which clearly she hadn't.

Not wishing to dwell too long on this legal issue, it is relevant to the unfolding story that I refused to accept this local ruling and was bold enough to seek out Graham when he came on duty shortly thereafter. Graham, perfectly sober, listened to the arguments, weighed up the potential damage to his relationship with his CIO colleagues and decided to back me in what was to become a landmark case in the context of immigration law. The case went to the ultimate immigration court of appeal in London and resulted, after much legal argument, in a verdict to uphold the decision to refuse entry on the over-riding ground of primary purpose, which subsequently became enshrined in law.

Unbeknown to me, this legal milestone had also come to the attention of Another Government Department, whose senior officers considered that the judgement might have beneficial implications for dealing with foreign nationals of threat to the security of the State. An immigration officer's power of detention was then and continues to be, in theory anyway, limitless and does not rely on the person being formally charged or tried, as is the case within the criminal code.

This led to my MI6 file being reopened and to another meeting with Hayden, who was by then very close to retirement.

Out of the blue, but some time later, I received a telephone call from Hayden suggesting a rendezvous the next day at a pub near Victoria station. Clearly, Hayden had established that I was not required to be at work that day and perhaps even knew I had no other pressing engagements.

Given the length of time since our last meeting and my growing unease with the loose and undefined relationship I had with Hayden and his covert Department, there was no real enthusiasm for agreeing to the request. In fact, I felt hugely nervous about the whole business and wished to be rid of this special attention from a world about which I had no real knowledge. Another side of me, however, was curious and hungry enough to overcome this fear, the upshot of which was a British Rail day-return to London (to be reimbursed with interest courtesy of MI6).

CHAPTER 6

Not wishing to appear over-keen, I deliberately dressed down for the occasion, not least because it was an extremely hot summer's day, which brought out the sexiest dress sense, meaning minimalistic, in London's female population and sometimes the worst (behaviour) by their male counterparts. Hey ho!, I thought, it was only going to be yet another prick-teasing session in the company of an old man with nothing better to do with his time than make vague promises, with no intention of delivering the goods, to a young hopeful with no idea of what he wanted from him.

Carnations were not required to bring the two interlocutors together. We were known to one another, though I had grown several inches and Hayden had aged by more than the six years since our last we met.

"Dear boy, how you have changed. Has life been kind to you and what plans have you for the future? I have to confess that my own plans are somewhat limited by dint of the aging process. Anno Domini and all that twaddle, don't you know."

I took this to be an opening ploy, rather in the way I used to tempt chess opponents into a false sense of confidence before delivering the *coup de main* leading to the toppling of their King.

"I'm just fine, thank you. I have a wife, a good job and, I believe, reasonable prospects."

"Excellent, I would have expected no less of you. Time moves on, Old Boy, and it behoves you to move with it. Let me come to the point. Our department has kept a fatherly eye on you over the last several years and we have decided to make you an offer we hope you won't refuse. We would like you to work for us as an undeclared agent in a country that might surprise you. It is labelled the largest democracy in the world and, to some degree, this is a fair description. However, we are aware of political developments that might well result in a regime less well disposed to HMG than the current one. How would you like to be posted to India ostensibly as an immigration attaché on secondment to the F&CO and, at the same time, do a bit of snooping for MI6? I'm not talking James Bond, more "One of our undercover people in the sub-Continent. What do you say?"

I was gobsmacked to receive such a direct and off-the wall proposal, yet at the same time I was elated that my talents had at last been acknowledged at the highest level. I was not at all sure that the faith and confidence placed in me was justified in the great scheme of things, but I knew I possessed the will power to return the compliment with interest.

"Can I ask you, Sir, what the risks are and what protection there will be for me and my family?", I asked with genuine interest.

"All taken care of by the department. Don't give it another thought – we always bring our warriors home alive", (when we can, I almost heard). "Your duties will be low-key, not at all dangerous and not very demanding. In exchange, we shall reimburse you most generously to the point you will feel no pain."

I rejoined: "So, what and with whom do you expect me to do business?". Hayden moved conspiratorially closer to me and whispered in my ear words that did not inspire me with confidence and that I would never forget.

"The fact is, young man, that we currently have a real problem with the Indian Central Intelligence Bureau (IB), which refuses to do business with us as openly as we would like. Not sure why - we gave them a legacy built on the British model, never bettered, and all we ask in return is an accurate and regular report of their dealings with their nearest and dearest. Pakistan has become bit of a bête noir in recent times and is on track to be much, much worse in years to come. We need to keep a tight rein on both of them lest they move in directions we would not like." As a rider, he added, "And there's also the complication of bloody Bangladesh. Excuse my language, but the country has become somewhat of an undesirable complication despite its laudable aspirations since gaining self-rule and independence in 1971."

The conversation seemed to have its own momentum - well rehearsed on the part of Hayden and emotionally overwhelming on my part. One drink led to another and my reluctance to come on board lessened accordingly.

Hayden, with a stroke of sheer genius, reeled his man in with the words: "Let's say you are yet to be convinced, but that you are interested to the point that you would like to know more. Perhaps you would agree to a short introductory course at the factory, yes?"

I knew I could not refuse an offer I had been hoping for, but did not dare to expect, and therefore gave a nod of affirmation.

"Top man, young Dai, the department will be in touch with you soon to agree a time and date."

CHAPTER 7

The time and date followed relatively quickly, and I found myself one wet, Monday morning in 1974 at a small SIS office near St. James' underground station. Hayden, looking every inch the Oxbridge professor – indeed, had achieved a Classics double First from Oxford - was there to introduce me to his instructors, made his apologies for not being able to stay, then curiously left the premises without saying farewell.

The induction lasted the whole day and included a complete one-to-one briefing on the Indian Intelligence Bureau (IB) and the Pakistan directorate for Inter-Service Intelligence (usually referred to as the ISI).

I found the subject matter most interesting despite not fully picking-up on all the political and military nuances that surrounded it. I learned that the IB is reputed to be the oldest intelligence agency in the world, that it was tasked with all intelligence targeting and that it fell under the Ministry of Home Affairs (MHA).

The collection, analysis and dissemination mechanisms of the IB vary depending on the region, but it was clear that it operated at both state and national level. The hierarchy was fairly primitive, relying on low-grade officers to make the initial running and for intelligence so gathered to move up the food chain depending on how it is assessed by its monitors. Grade II officers, the majority, are in part drawn from direct recruitment, whereas Grade I officers are mostly drawn from state services.

The IB maintains a large number of field units, which, like its headquarters, are under the control of Joint or Deputy Directors. It is through these offices that the intricate process of deputation and the 'organic' linkage between the state police agencies and the IB is maintained. Unlike its UK or US equivalents, the IB was not financially attractive to its agents and, as a result, did not attract, at that time, top quality, career intelligence officers but, rather, relied on 'forced' transfers from the various Indian police forces to make up its numbers.

The IB was the Government of India's principal news agency (read propaganda machine) and was responsible for reviewing all aspects of governance. At the central level, the IB closely monitored developments relating to parliamentary affairs and reported back to the Cabinet Secretariat. Its critics claimed that this role was more to do with targeting political opponents. What's new in the world of politics?

In matters of counter-intelligence operations, the IB has attracted even more criticism, more information on which would follow at subsequent briefings.

As for the Pakistanis, the ISI was established in 1948 (as Pakistan engaged India in the first war over Kashmir), and has since been accused of many vices. Critics say it runs 'a state within a state', subverts elected governments, supports the Taliban and is even involved in drug smuggling, all of which was and continued to be strenuously denied by Pakistan's government until the twenty-first century.

In the 1950s, when Pakistan joined anti-communist alliances, its military services and the ISI received considerable Western support in training and equipment. India was, of course, considered to be its arch enemy, and vice versa.

When Ayub Khan, the then army commander-in-chief, mounted the first successful coup in 1958, the ISI's domestic, political activities expanded. As a new state bringing together diverse ethnic groups within what some pundits described as contrived borders, Pakistan faced separatist challenges from Pashtuns, Balochis, Sindhis and Bengalis. What is certain is that the ISI is a military intelligence provider and is a central organ of Pakistan's military machine, which has played a major, sometimes dominant role in the country's often turbulent politics. The ISI not only mounted surveillance on parties and politicians, it often infiltrated, co-opted, cajoled or coerced them into supporting the army's centralisation agenda.

Following the creation of Bangladesh in 1971, the ISI and the military were thoroughly discredited and marginalised after the war, only gaining fresh purpose in 1972 when Zulfiqar Ali Bhutto, the new civilian leader, launched a clandestine project to build nuclear weapons. A year later military operations were launched against nationalist militants in Balochistan province. These two events helped to rehabilitate both the ISI and the military.

What was to unfold 3 years' later would find me in a situation almost exactly opposite to that described by Hayden as 'low-key, not at all dangerous and not very demanding'.

CHAPTER 8

Thus the indoctrination process was almost complete. Like the proverbial salmon, I was well and truly hooked. It was just a matter of time before I was landed. The question was, would I be compliant or would I wriggle and fight on the line?

I considered my options and decided a life in the murky waters of unspoken secrecy was preferable to the mundane, day-to-day existence that caused me such angst and frustration as a boy soldier in the regular Civil Service.

But, in reality, what did this under-cover existence really mean in terms of self-preservation, peace of mind and career advancement? Outwardly, it offered an almost glamorous persona imbued with all the trappings of being a secret squirrel.

At the same time, I had to balance my day-job with my covert aspirations, and, in doing so, had to maintain a normal family life-style, which meant doing what I did best without giving rise to unwanted suspicion. Fortunately, Rhiannon was more interested in family and domestic responsibilities and, as a consequence, gave me a relatively easy time.

My first task was to establish myself as a competent visa officer (called entry certificate officer in Commonwealth countries) in Bombay (now Mumbai), which, at the time, was not without its problems. There were but four immigration attachés in post - 2 Foreign & Commonwealth Office (F&CO) and 2 Immigration Service (IS) – doing the workload of six. The locally engaged staff were hugely helpful and supportive, having seen a succession of the good, bad and the ugly UK staff over a period of several years. Fortunately, my IS colleague was a man of serious aptitude, humour and intelligence. Far more than that, Bob was my touchstone, my stable mate and personified the high standard of professionalism to which I could only aspire. The two F&CO officers were pleasant enough, but initially lacked the basic immigration skills to do the job without major input from their IS gurus. The upshot of this was that I found I had much less time for my alter ego than I would have liked or, indeed, needed in terms of devoting quality time to my night job.

One very pleasant diversion from the pressures of both offices was an unexpected visit from one of the most esteemed and charismatic immigration officers to have found himself on the Indian sub-Continental scene. I knew nothing of Rick until the telegram arrived from the DHC in Calcutta announcing his imminent arrival. It had been addressed to Bob, who knew him, but who was unable to facilitate his short-term stay for reasons I cannot quite remember.

Anyway, from the tone of his telegram and from what Bob had imparted to me, I liked the cut of Rick's jib and decided to form a welcoming party, which consisted of me and one of my F&CO colleagues. The outcome of this arrangement was a most enjoyable evening at my club, the Bombay Gymkhana, and one that I shall never forget. Rick, then and now, is a natural raconteur, regaled us with stories, which, if only faintly true, were rivetingly funny.

In fact, it took several months for the imbedding process to elapse, during which time I took the opportunity of studying the Deputy High Commission's (DHC) personnel, working practices and resident MI6 'friend', who was well and truly declared and whose apparent dysfunctional appearance disguised a sharp and acutely observant mover and shaker. Said agent knew only the very minimum of information about my presence at the mission, but enough to afford me the right level of support and assistance I would require over the next few years. In the event, this was to prove crucial.

One of the features of life as an attaché was the opportunity to take field trips to the hinterland; in Bombay's case this meant Gujarat State, the home of Mahatma Ghandi and one of India's most prolific exporters of humankind, most notably to east Africa and the UK. I made a field trip in the late summer of 1976 to Ahmadabad and the university city of Baroda (known locally as Vadodra), with a couple of en route visits to villages and towns, most notably the Islamic communities of Surat and Broach, known to be problematic to the UK immigration control. The headman (sarpanch) in Surat took great delight in offering me and my interpreter, Mr GM Bhutt a welcoming drink. I was schooled not to ask for pani (water) or buruff (ice) and opted, instead, for a Cola.

"So sorry, sahib, Cola we are not having. And before you ask, we are similarly not having any fizzy drinks for your choice of beverage. So sorry indeed."

The slow, lateral movement of the head and the look of *Schadenfreude* in his eyes convinced me that I was about to receive a severe dose of Montezuma's revenge. In the end and knowing how important it was not to give offence, I opted for a glass of milk, which offer, mistakenly as it turned out, received a nod of the head from Mr GM Bhutt. What emerged before us was a most unattractive glass of thick, warm, grey-white liquid with protruding hairs, including a dollop of black ice. 'Hey ho', I thought, 'This is Moslem pay-back day. Lie back and think of Wales'.

On our arrival in Ahmadabad, we discovered that our hotel booking had been cancelled because of an incoming group of rich and important Gujarati businessmen (such is India). This led to Mr GM Bhutt and me having to book into the local Circuit House (Chottu, the driver, taking up his normal sleeping position in the car), which was reasonably priced and comfortable enough. Because it was nearly full, I had to share a room with Mr GM Bhutt, much to the latter's huge embarrassment. My constitution had already been weakened in Bombay by a serious bout of amoebic dysentery, the recollection of which caused me to take immediate, remedial action. This was a bottle of scotch placed handily on my bedside table. Mr GM Bhutt, a devout Brahmin, was moved to utter a few mantras whilst I tucked into my third burra peg. The next morning I felt on top of the world, unlike Mr GM Bhutt who was very ill indeed, and remained so for the next 3 days. On a previous trip to Ahmadabad I had been an honoured guest at the festival of Makar Sacranti, which includes aerial kite battles of almost savage dimensions and which is held every year on 14 January.

In Baroda, particularly, I made several good contacts, some of whom had been expelled from Uganda by the appalling Idi Amin in the early seventies. There was, of course, the inevitable UK visa element to the otherwise splendid, not to say generous reception. The fact remained that I was introduced to some big players in the Patel community, including senior politicians, industrialists and professionals, some of whom would, of right, later settle in the UK and become fast friends.

It just so happened that I had been assigned more trips than anyone else in the DHC and that I did not always confine myself to the published itinerary. The cover was perfect in that the actual and the covert could seamlessly be blended to the point that no-one would suspect the reasons for the unexpected change of plan that required me to become separated from my driver and interpreter for a couple of days. Subsequently, I was tasked with making 5 visits to Gujarat in less than 3 weeks in order to find the perfect village for the then Prime Minister, James Callaghan to casually drop in on and ostensibly to chat with happy Gujaratis who had made their fortune in the UK and had returned to their native land to invest lavishly in the local community. Suffice to say, it did not take long to establish that no such village existed and for the one I did eventually identify to cause a diplomatic incident. The PM swept in with his retinue, met the village elders, said a few kind words of encouragement about co-operative farming and, as he was about to leave, was verbally berated and almost physically attacked by the local 'madman', who had indeed been to the UK and who had been temporarily locked-up for the duration of the visit. Regrettably, he had escaped his confines in time to tell Jim a thing or two and then some. When the PM returned to Bombay as a guest of the pompous Deputy High Commissioner at his (then) impressive residence, Jinnah House, I found myself relegated to guarding the office Chancery with nothing to lift me other than a home-made tomato sandwich, which my cook, never having made one before, had prepared by placing a whole tomato between two pieces of bread. Not one of my best days, I have to say.

Returning to the summer of 1976, my first SIS commission was to feign illness and make a diversionary flight from Ahmadabad, via Delhi, to one of India's restricted areas. Everything had been laid on by the SIS, which provided me with ample funds, return air tickets, government of India permission to enter one of their more sensitive hot spots and an outline briefing on what I needed to know and achieve whilst there. So far, so good.

That destination was one of India's more sparsely populated regions called Ladakh, which is situated in the northern state of Jammu and Kashmir and which is commonly referred to, for very good reason, as 'the Land of High Passes'. What an eye-opener that was, both literally and metaphorically. Historically, Ladakh, was the connection post between central and south Asia when the Silk Road was in use. The sixty day journey on the route connecting Amritsar and Yarkland through eleven passes was frequently undertaken by traders until the third quarter of the nineteenth century. These traditional routes have been closed since the Ladakh-Tibetan border was sealed by the Chinese government. Shit happens. The region lies between the Kunlon mountain range in the north and the great Himalayas to the south, inhabited by people of Indo-Aryan and Tibetan descent, and is sometimes called 'Little Tibet'.

The plane landed rather erratically at a small airport near the regional capital of Leh, which sits 3500 metres above sea level and lies just north of the river Indus. Getting down at Leh, the traveller is primarily moved by a single emotion. Yes, his eyes, he feels, are much too small; the altitude combined with the absolute purity of the air, the mountains of varied colours seemingly covered with a sheet of steel, cut through a blue of an intensity dreamed up by a serene goddess. I was met on the runway by my named contact, Vikram Singh, whose role in the great scheme of things had been explained to me in sufficient detail, but no more, to make informed decisions. The special reception attracted a deal of interest from the rest of the passengers, not unusual in the Indian sub-Continent, but otherwise passed without lasting memory.

Vikram and I were driven at high speed in a blacked-out Ambassador car to a location in Leh that was clearly under the control of the Indian Central Intelligence Bureau (IB). My briefing was to keep my ears open and my mouth shut, and, at the first opportunity, to relay the intelligence so gathered to a pre-arranged destination point in New Delhi.

I was aware that Vikram earned far more money working for MI6 than he did from his state employer, that he was not a supporter of India's move towards becoming a nuclear power and that he had been tasked by his London masters to take me into the hinterland for the purpose of acquiring intelligence on India's nuclear aspirations.

The Leh address was, in fact, an IB safe-house to which Vikram had easy access. The Indian Airlines flight from Delhi had not been a pleasant one, so the Scotch whisky, Burra peg naturally, was gratefully received and soon replenished with even more fingers.

Once Vikram was satisfied that I was reasonably relaxed, he provided me with a presentation on the current state of play in Ladakh and on the potential for intelligence gathering.

CHAPTER 9

Vikram's rehearsed pitch was:

"In the 1950s, India acquired nuclear technologies aimed to encourage civil use of nuclear energy as part of the 'Atoms for Peace' non-proliferation programme. Little interest was revealed in developing nuclear weapons until India successfully detonated a nuclear device in May 1974. The test was described by the government of India as a peaceful nuclear explosion."

What was not known at the time was that later, in the 1980s, India began research on thermonuclear weapon capability and then conducted operation Shatkri, which amounted to a series of 5 nuclear detonations. A few weeks later, Pakistan tested 5 nuclear devices of its own, the sum total of which was that both countries were then nuclear powers, but clearly not on the same side.

Vikram then moved into real-world speak, as he understood it. The whisky was beginning to take affect, despite which I remained acutely alert and attentive. Vikram explained the territorial problems of the region and altitude, which encompasses desolate moonscapes, wastelands and snow-capped mountains cold enough to freeze your bollocks off. The landscape changes from the fertile green valleys of Kashmir to the bare hillsides of Central Asia.

To the north of Leh is a road that seems never to stop rising ever higher on an astral quest. This is the Beacon Highway, which is the highest road in the world. Khardong La shows us a forbidden valley called Nubra. Here the Siachen meets the Shayok, which is remarkably green in contrast with the rest of Ladakh.

The inhabitants of Nubra offer to the modern traveller the hospitality reserved in earlier times for the caravans on the silk road, which came to this rich oasis to replenish their supplies. The region is a favourite of ornithologists throughout the globe, who go there (permits permitting) to see some of the rarest birds known to man. This was my cover story. If only they had realised how little I knew about the feathered variety. On average, the temperature varies between minus 3 degrees to plus 30 degrees Centigrade in the summer, and to minus 15 degrees to minus 20 degrees in the winter. At the time of my visit, the temperature was much nearer 3 degrees Centigrade than 30.

So what was the attraction by the government of India to this beautiful, but remote and unforgiving part of the world? Vikram took a gulp of his whisky before hesitantly imparting intelligence of the highest, not to say most personally dangerous classification.

"You will be aware, Dai that my country pursues an entirely reciprocal, some would say paranoiac campaign against Pakistan, a legacy of 1947 and the atrocities on both sides that accompanied it, and that it will do everything within its power to nullify the threat posed by Pakistan's mainstream politicians and its extreme Islamic fundamentalists, especially in the area of territorial protectionism, Kashmir, of course, being the powder-keg.

You will also have been briefed on the 'peaceful' development of nuclear advancement that both countries publically annunciate. Your intelligence people know as well as I do that this is complete and utter claptrap. What we would like to do to one-another defies description and has not changed since the abominations of Partition. The culprit, as usual, is religion, or, more accurately, the lack of adherence to the tenets of what are both true religions, which is or has been a serial killer in so many parts of the world such as Israel against the rest of the Middle East and vice versa; Northern Ireland Protestants against anything wearing a Catholic badge, and the obverse by the IRA and its army of thugs in equal measure; Turkey's understandable obsession with nullifying Kurdistan nationalist ambitions; Middle Eastern Sunnis verses Shiites, etcetera, etcetera.

The bottom line, as your masters in London already know - and which is why you are here- is that there are senior rogue elements within the IB who are actively planning to hold underground nuclear explosions not 150 miles from where we are now sitting. The word on the ground is that they have already detonated a nuclear device, more of which later.

Our mission is initially to observe and report and, ultimately, to prevent this from happening by whatever means are available to us, which, frankly, are currently not too encouraging. The bad news is that we have an early start, the slightly worse news is that I am still working on a game-plan."

I slept very badly that night, not surprisingly, and was woken at 5am by the gentle shake of my arm by a man not known to me, but whose physical appearance, even in the dusk before the dawn chorus, was awesome. He was well over two metres tall, was clearly, from his dress and demeanour, a Sikh and possessed the look of a man who did not take prisoners. Kuldip Singh was an IB 'enforcer', who was familiar with the local terrain and who knew how to move around Ladakh without leaving a traceable foot-print in the snow. I knew from information imparted to me by my Bombay friend, Jaideep that 'all Sikhs are Singhs, but not all Singhs are Sikhs'. As Michael Cane might say: 'not a lot of people know that'.

Breakfast was mercifully light and conversation was equally minimalistic. The latter, on reflection, worried me more than somewhat, given that this was my first assignment and because I had only the barest outline of why I was here. Vikram had laid on appropriate, well-fitting clothes and the necessary transport, which consisted of two super-charged motorised rickshaws, the larger one to be driven by Kuldip and the other solo by one of Kuldip's many, but otherwise unnamed 'brothers'. I noticed that it contained a number of boxes and wondered what they were. None of us carried anything that could identify a corpse. For those of you unfamiliar with this form of Eastern transport, the pulled rickshaw has two wheels and travels at between 4 and 7 miles an hour, depending what the hirer is prepared to pay. The motorised version moves at around 20 miles an hour and has three wheels. The super-charged one that I was to board had a top speed of sixty miles an hour, which felt a lot faster in the doing.

The journey out of Leh took us to the Beacon Highway, on which we travelled in a northerly direction for several hours. The further away from Leh we progressed the bleaker the scenery became. I felt we could have been on another planet, for which I had no parameters or geographical benchmarks. We covered long distances without seeing another vehicle, until, that is, three very distinctive Indian army trucks passed us at great speed. I noticed a surprised exchange of eye contact between Vikram and Kuldip. The ever-increasing altitude did nothing for my ears, which popped rather painfully from time to time.

Not long afterwards, Kuldip signalled to Vikram that they were fast approaching our destination, which turned out to be nothing out of the ordinary. The location had been chosen by Vikram and Kuldip because it afforded a good view of the terrain that intelligence suggested was the likely site of their scrutiny. I noted the valley below and the mountain above, without any recognition of their relevance to the task in hand.

Vikram put me out of my misery. "Dai, you look confused, and why shouldn't you? I have been researching the Ladakh project for some time and have adduced developments that lead me to believe we are in the right area to point our equipment. You will have seen the boxes in the other rickshaw and you are about to learn what they contain."

On that note, Kuldip appeared on the scene with his 'brother', both carrying the boxes that were quickly unpacked, revealing an array of electronic devices not familiar to me in any shape, way or form. In no time at all, they were activated and directed towards an area just south of a range of high ground that did not appear to me to have any unusual features, which, of course, was why it had been chosen in the first place.

I ventured to ask what, exactly, was being measured, and Vikram responded by saying that the equipment was highly sensitive and would detect any sign of recent nuclear activity. He went on to say: "I should add that we need to move very quickly to avoid the focus of unwanted attention. You saw the military trucks that passed us on the Beacon Highway. I know of no scheduled movements that would require their presence at this moment in time. I may have missed something, but I am naturally a cautious man to the point that we should assume that our cover has been blown, or, at least, exposed to military curiosity."

Fifteen minutes later, Vikram examined the initial results from a sort of tickertape read-out, asked Kuldip to re-box the equipment using the familiar Hindi expression 'Jeldi, jeldi man!', meaning in this context: 'before your arse catches fire!'

My heart was pumping for Wales, and for very good reason. We all heard the increasingly loud sound of approaching vehicles, reminiscent of the army trucks that had passed us earlier and correctly assumed that we were the targets of their attention.

Before you could say 'Mahatma Gandhi', the two rickshaws were retreating hell for leather back toward Leh. The precious instrumentation had displaced Kuldip in the larger rickshaw, and the two 'brothers' followed in the smaller one.

An exchange of instructions led to Kuldip taking pole position and to Vikram taking his vehicle off-road to be hidden in a small copse that would not easily be found in such an otherwise arid environment. Minutes later – my heart was beating even faster with a pulse rate that would have registered at least ten on the Richter scale – we heard a rapid burst of gunfire and the noise of a vehicle crashing into something very hard.

Moments late there was a buzzing aerial noise that signalled the presence of one or more helicopters, which moved over the target zone like circling vultures.

The pursuers had made a hit, but were not at all sure they had fulfilled their military orders. The subsequent search for a second vehicle drew a blank, and the Indian army pursuers returned to base camp to, face a probably very angry and unhappy senior officer.

An hour or so later and in the knowledge that my flight back to Delhi was just 5 hours away, Vikram decided that the immediate threat was over and so decided that we should return to Leh without further delay. We observed the second rickshaw in a mangled state, but there was no sign of our two Sikh colleagues. I wondered if they had been taken alive and, if so, if were they being interrogated (or worse)? This question I assumed to be crucial to the outcome of the mission and to the lifespan of the two captured agents, assuming they were alive. Given that there was no room for manoeuvre on the one and only road back to the capital, we had to place their fate and destiny – kismet as it is known in Islamic countries – in the hands of the gods. Luckily, as it turned out, the gods were on our side and we arrived, tired and dispirited, at the safe-house without further grief.

There was not much time or appetite for a proper debriefing and, after eating a hurried meal, Vikram drove me to the airport with the promise of early contact via 'the usual channels'. I noticed a faint look of fear, or could that have been pity, on Vikram's face, an image that was to stay with me for the whole of my return journey, which turned out to be even more traumatic than the outward one.

The plane took off on time and was fairly full. I was emotionally exhausted and fell asleep within minutes of take-off. My REM dream, however, was fitful and must have unnerved the person in the next seat, a large Rajasthan woman, who wrongly assumed the 'foreigner' must have had too much to drink. After reaching its target height, the plane began to wobble a bit, followed by the more extreme affects of turbulence caused by the onset of the return monsoon and the air displacement it created. I felt the change of mood in the cabin staff and took out my one week-old copy of the Daily Telegraph. By the time I realised the knuckles of my hands were white and the paper was upside down, the aircraft was dropping at an alarming rate, just falling out of the sky without anything to stop it. Many of my fellow passengers were screaming uncontrollably as the plane continued to plummet several thousand feet and also to oscillate like a leaf in the wind. I wondered how much worse it could get before I met my maker. All of a sudden the plane made a loud banging sound, levelled out as if nothing had happened and continued its journey to Delhi.

The plane landed well enough, but my legs, as I descended the steps, were like jelly, a condition that would take several days to right. I was now a much troubled man and it was not at all clear if or how I would recover my equilibrium. I took a taxi to my rendezvous point, was met by an SIS agent and provided with the means of writing my report, which I duly did before making my way back to the airport.

CHAPTER 10

On my return to Ahmadabad, I was physically and emotionally drained. I had lost half a stone in weight, but had significantly developed my skills as an SIS agent. In short, I had come of age.

I became reunited with my team of two, who were far too polite to ask where I had been for the last two days. The road journey back to Bombay was slow and unrewarding, largely due to the heavy traffic, but mainly as a result of my scrambled state of mind. This was the first real lesson I had had in managing my double life, which I realised I could share with no-one, including my wife. I felt very lonely indeed.

It did not take long, however, for me to rediscover the joys of my day job and the normality of family life. Rhiannon was most impressed with the quality of the Gujarati mirror-work I had expensively bought for her in Ahmadabad and the DHC was pleased to read my report, especially the bits that covered my meetings with the great and the good in Baroda. Doubtless, this was passed on to London SW1A by the DHC as 'all his own work'. No matter, I had written my more important report, which I later learned had been well received by Another Government Department and its close ally, for which read the CIA.

I imagined that the enormity of my product was to set alarm bells ringing in London and Washington for some time to come. Both organisations had known that India was developing nuclear weapons and that Pakistan was not far behind them. What I assumed they did not know was just how far the former had progressed over the last year or so, the ramifications of which were almost as politically galvanising as the ones flowing from the long-running cold war with the Soviet union. It would not be long before I received my next commission.

A happy diversion was the arrival in Bombay of the 1976 MCC team, which was chaperoned by the Bombay British Consul, John Donald Shannon (JDS), who was and remains one of my best friends and whose pedigree for the cricketing job was second to none. This proved to be a memorable and happy diversion from the traumas of my trip to Ladakh. Captain John 'Mike' Brearley's team was extremely gifted in every department of the game, as was evidenced by their excellent results, both at provincial and international level. The side included such luminaries as John Lever, Chris Old, Bob Willis, Alan Knott, the inimitable Derek William Randall (also known as Arkle), probably the best out fielder England, and arguably the rest of the world has ever seen, and many others of equal quality. And JDS ensured that they enjoyed the many and varied attractions of the Indian sub-Continent to the full. He was born to the task and delivered a first class job, which was hugely appreciated by the whole team, players and managers alike. John and his gregarious and multi-talented wife, Stella made the 'Boys' feel at home and protected them from some of the pitfalls that await the uninitiated on their first visit to the sub-Continent.

One of my abiding memories was of an evening spent at the Deputy High Commissioner's luxurious residence, Jinnah House, where the MCC party members were the guests of honour. The house itself was a colonial mansion that had been owned by Muhammad Ali Jinnah , the founding father of Pakistan, who bequeathed it to the British government around the time of the 1947 Partition (only for the government of India to subsequently translate 'gift' into a peppercorn rent, which it increased hugely in the late seventies, leading to the F&CO moving its DHC into much reduced accommodation and to the gardens and house falling into complete disrepair). It boasted a splendid marble patio area, with steps leading down to one of the best gardens in Bombay, and on which certain elements of the MCC players decided to build a pyramid of empty Tennants lager cans, doubtless encouraged by the mischievous JDS. The DHC was not sportingly inclined and did not see the funny side of what was inevitably to follow. One of the cans was removed from its supporting base position, which caused the rest to fall from grace in a cacophony of tin on marble and which triggered the ear-shattering cheers of those responsible. Wonderful stuff and just the tonic I needed. The evening ended when JDS was found fast asleep in one of the many rose bushes of Jinnah House with a smile on his face that spoke wonders for the accumulative festivities of the night.

Life went on in the immigration section of the office as usual, two paces forward, three back; more importantly big political events were taking place in India under the Prime Ministership of the formidable Indirha Gandhi, who had declared an Emergency situation in her early tenure at the helm. This was an unusual political era in terms of political gender, which historically has been, and continues to be, male dominated. Here we had Indirha in charge of the biggest democracy in the world, Margaret Thatcher as the then head of the Conservative party and future PM and Golda Meir as PM of Israel until 1974. One of the more grabbing headlines in the Times of India at the time was 'The Iron Lady (Margaret Thatcher) meets the Steel Butterfly' (Indirha Ghandi). Wonderful, wonderful stuff.

The Emergency saw thousands of beggars being rounded up in the main conurbations and transported to the outreaches of the countryside, only for the bulk of them to return a few weeks later, by one means or another including skayeboards, to the very spots from where they had been abducted.

It also saw large numbers of government servants being ordered to improve their daily attendance rate, which resulted in the embarrassing situation of there being many more workers than desks and seats and the inevitable consequence of the overflow being sent home because their working environments could not physically accommodate them. If nothing else, this demonstrated just how long this malpractice had been allowed to continue and how unprepared the government was effectively to deal with it.

CHAPTER 11

Another diversion for me was the game of Rugby Union. As a member of the prestigious Bombay Gymkhana Club, I regularly played football, snooker, badminton and squash, but my main contribution to the club was as skipper of the rugby team.

The Gymkhana had not won the All India and South Asia Rugby Tournament for many years and was very keen to put this to rights. The competition was played alternatively in Bombay and Calcutta. In 1977 it was Bombay's turn to host the event, which was made up of sixteen teams, depending on the availability of players, many of whom were police officers.

Centre stage was the legendary Callaghan of India, whose real name was RW Leybourne Callaghan, formerly skipper of Dublin Wanderers and then currently the Asian CEO of a major international pharmaceutical company. RWL was one of those larger than life characters, who would have done justice to a key role in a John Le Carré novel (possibly as the flamboyant father figure, who is possibly, and I mean only possibly reincarnated in his latest novel: 'A most wanted man'). Though in his early sixties, Callaghan of India still played the game when he wasn't refereeing and continued to boast a strong physique and the sweet tongue of an Irish poet. His house parties were never dull and usually ended up with Leybourne wrestling his head bearer on the lounge carpet. This same bearer was charged with awakening his master every morning, around 5am, by placing an ice-cube on each of his eyes. His standard ware, from which he rarely departed, was a crisp, dark suit, an immaculately white shirt, always with a tie, and a red rose in his lapel. Eccentric but memorable.

Leybourne was also a mover and shaker of monumental proportions and had the gift of the gab in spades, a talent he often employed to prevent some of the Gymkhana's less than friendly committee members from taking less than friendly club decisions that were not conducive to the rugby section (or any other section that Leybourne supported). He was a master of his craft, a most astute man and someone whom I held in awe and complete respect, particularly the likable rogue element of his personality.

More than that, Leybourne was the consummate businessman, whose talents ranged from making day-to-day Bombay deals to those more associated with that of a global entrepreneur.

His close ally was another engaging man by the name of Sarosh Nagarvala, known affectionately to his friends as 'Buggerwalla', who was pivotal to the Gymkhana rugby section and who had perfected the art of the trailing leg and the late tackle. His father, Jimmy, had been a senior Maharashtran police officer, who successfully investigated the assassination of Mahatma Ghandi. Sarosh's claim to fame was as an international ice hockey referee and commentator at a time when the Indian ground hockey team ranked as the best in the world, the country having won an astonishing 8 Olympic gold medals between 1952 and 1980. In fact, 7 of the squad that won the 1976 gold medal were Gymkhana members, which meant that the club was immensely strong and almost impossible to beat. Both he and RWL were marked men whenever they came up against a Calcutta side, especially the Armenian team, which bore Lebourne a huge grudge because of an alleged misdemeanour that no-one could actually remember. This was graphically illustrated when he played against them in the 1978 'All India' in Calcutta. Well before half-time, Leybourne had found himself the victim of gross Armenian GBH tactics, which resulted in his face looking like a butcher's cutting-board. I ordered him to leave the pitch to receive medical attention, a Captain's decision which he steadfastly refused to obey. He saw the game out and emerged all the stronger for it and, quite rightly, immensely proud of his achievement .

Other luminaries in the 1977 victory were my very good friends, Pesh Framji and Alan Samuel, the former from an established Parsi family and the latter from a most respectable Anglo-Indian family, both of whom we had the privilege of socialising with. Pesh, now a senior UK chartered accountant with a global reputation in charity and World Wild Life work, was, in his youth, as mad as a hatter. He kept snakes in his bedroom and made an alcoholic concoction that would have seen off a troop of Russian Cossacks in no time at all. His saving grace was his girlfriend, now wife, Yasmin, who kept him on the straight and narrow. Alan was a gifted rugby player, who could have played at a much higher level had circumstances been different. Another of my rugby chums was a Frenchman, equally as mad as Pesh, called Michel Sabatier. He had graduated from one of France's top echelon educational institutions and had, as a consequence, been given a position as a French diplomat in Bombay instead of being drafted into the French Foreign Legion. Michel was a multi-talented fellow, who had a strong feeling for and empathy with the Indian sub-Continent, married the beautiful and equally clever Berhoze , but never quite ran as fast as I did, much to his chagrin. There were many others, too numerous to mention, but collectively they all contributed to my leaving India with a warm feeling of brotherhood.

The 'All India' cup stands over two feet high and was donated by the RFU in return for the Calcutta Football and Cricket Club's (CFCC) generosity in providing the silverware (cutlery and rupees) that was melted down and used to make the Calcutta Cup, which is presented annually to the winners of the England- Scotland six nations rugby match. The history of the cup stems from a game played on Christmas Day 1872 at the emerging Calcutta Football Club ground between 20 Englishmen against the same number of Scottish, Welsh and Irish rugby players.

Thanks to some wheeling and dealing by Leybourne and Sarosh, the Gym's 1977 side included the best players from the local Wilson College squad, which had handsomely won the title in Calcutta in1976. The Bombay competition received widespread coverage by the local and national Indian media, including television and cinema as well as the main English language newspaper – the Times of India. It came as no surprise, therefore, that the Gym were the winning finalists. The same tactic was attempted in 1978, but I vetoed it because I considered it wholly unfair to Wilson College, whose players deserved better. Despite having to play its matches with its normal squad (apart from the late acquisition of a junior Welsh and New Zealand international, the less said about which the better), the Bombay Gymkhana went on to retain the cup by beating said CFCC by a try to nil in the final, which ended in almost complete darkness. This was only a few months before I and my family, which now included two sons, were to return to Blighty shortly before Christmas 1978, having spent slightly over 3 years in the enigma wrapped in a puzzle known as India.

CHAPTER 12

Prior to my end of tour, I was to experience an SIS commission of nightmarish proportions.

The contact was made by means of a high level, encrypted 'For Your Eyes Only' dispatch from London, via the local Bombay Chancery. No-one in the Chancery was used to receiving such a communication, and there followed a great deal of interest and speculation as to why it had been personally addressed to me. As it turned out, this was a major error on the part of a junior London SIS cipher officer, who had not realised the importance of my anonymity and whose career was foreshortened accordingly.

There followed a flurry of to and fro activity between London and Bombay, culminating in a final **'or else'** threat to protect the communication's content and that of its intended recipient. No-one argued, the DHC cipher clerk was sworn to secrecy and the Deputy High Commissioner was, for very good reason, not informed.

Once familiar with my tasking, I felt a distinct feeling of unease. My knee-jerk reaction was to distance myself from my commitment to the SIS. Inwardly I knew I had taken the Queen's shilling and that there was no way out. More importantly, I realised the distinction between bravery and bravado.

I knew that my involvement in the previous escapade had been nothing to do with anything I might have contributed as a specialist in my field; I also correctly inferred that my presence in Ladakh was more to do with India's neighbour, Pakistan.

Bull's Eye. The Ladakh mission could have been achieved without me being there at all. The only reason I had been invited to the party was to give me a taste of what was to follow and to provide me with an insight into detecting an underground nuclear explosion footprint.

The whole thing had been stage managed by the UK and Indian secret intelligence services. No-one had been tortured or killed, the Singh trio continued to ply their trade and the Indian nuclear weapon proliferation was allowed to move forward. My many speculations of the splendid job well done were embarrassingly consigned to the dustbin.

In the world of diplomacy, there exists an accepted method of transporting sensitive material from point A to point B. This is achieved by means of a Diplomatic Bag, which, subject to strict criteria of passage, is protected from Customs' scrutiny.

This usually requires the personal involvement of an accredited diplomat, who has to physically carry the 'Bag' onto and from the mode of transport, in this case the plane, without help or assistance from an unaccredited third party. Different rules apply to large and heavy items.

I was told that I needed 3 days (at least) to complete my tasking, was advised on what clothes to bring and where to go once I had discharged my diplomatic bag responsibility at the British High Commission in Delhi. As it transpired, the briefing took me to the same address, near the Red Fort, that I had reported to on my return from Ladakh.

To my immense surprise, I was met at the door by my old recruiter, Hayden, who, I thought, had retired long ago and whom I had not seen for 4 years. Once we were both comfortably seated, Hayden moved into auto-drive.

"How the devil are you, young man? I really didn't expect to see you again after our last meeting in London. The gods and my masters, however, dictated otherwise, and I now find myself, once again, as a humble and obedient servant of the Crown. I promise, though, that this is definitely my last outing, so I had better make it a good one.

You came through the Ladakh caper with honours, and let me apologise now for the deception, which I'm sure you have worked out for yourself. It was important to provide you with a taste of what was to come and to introduce you to the electronic gizmos that you will need to operate in Pakistan, which continues to cause us and our American allies great concern. It is too late to halt the nuclear proliferation in India, which we consider to be far more stable than its Islamic neighbour. Pakistan is a powder keg waiting to go off. Its only saving grace is its armed services, especially the Army, which will intervene when their top brass consider the elected politicians have over-stepped the mark.

What I have to say to you today runs contrary to my advice when last we met in London. Your mission, as I believe they say in that awful television programme, should you agree to accept it –and I paraphrase – will test your strengths to the full and is potentially very dangerous. If you elect to pull out now, no-one would blame you. Restricting nuclear proliferation is, arguably, the world's number one priority. We and the CIA have invested a great deal of money and effort in monitoring aspirant nations. You already know that India is well advanced in their nuclear programme, far too late, as I said, for us to reverse the process.

The other side of the coin is more difficult to reconcile, both politically and morally. Whatever India does, Pakistan follows. Current intelligence suggests that they are in an advanced state of preparation and that they may well have already detonated their first nuclear bomb. It also identifies where that might have taken place. The Pakistan government's position is quite clear: they have no intention of becoming a member of the so-called Nuclear Club. Full stop.

The driving force behind Pakistan's impetus to join that Club, however, is one Dr Abdul Mohammed Iqbal, who doubtless will be credited with being the father of Pakistan's nuclear weapons programme and who was a leading force in the newly created Directorate of Technical Development (DTD), an important and hugely secret section of the Pakistan Atomic Energy Commission (PAEC), which was formed only a couple of years ago.

Iqbal set out to create a new model of proliferation. He used centrifuge design blueprints and supplier lists of companies, stolen from a Dutch facility he had worked for, to launch Pakistan's nuclear weapons programme. In the process, it is thought that he might have started a clandestine model of trade in forbidden technologies outside formal government controls.

It is suspected that Iqbal has plans to utilise shell companies, clandestine procurement techniques, smuggling networks, false user-end certificates and middle men for the purchase of equipment and technologies that are on the export control lists of advanced industrial countries."

I absorbed this plethora of information with blinking disbelief. What on earth could this half-trained SIS agent accomplish in such an arena of corruption and deception. I interrupted Hayden's otherwise flawless briefing by firing the question: **"WHY ME?!"**

Hayden looked at me with a combination of fatherly concern and steely-eyed professionalism.

"The reason you were posted to India is that you would not be known in Pakistan, which I know you have never visited and which has no record or photograph of you.

My boy, have I ever let you down, and before you say 'yes', let me add the rider: in the sense that I have put your life at risk or involved you in anything that you did not sign-up to? I identified your talents more than 15 years' ago, went out on a limb to recruit you against, I have to say, the judgement of some of my peers and brought you into a world you were born for. I even brought some of your chess games to the attention of a colleague British Grand Master, who considered you had a talent well beyond your years and a thought process that was conducive to undercover work.

What more do you want me say? All you have to do is to sign one or two bits of paper, walk out of the door and return to the comfort of the Bombay Gymkhana, in which rugger capacity, by the bye, my sincerest congratulations."

I sat there with a very dry mouth for a short while, before saying to Hayden: "Don't get me wrong, I am up for this job, but I would like to know what, exactly, my role is and what my chances of survival are."

Another silence.

"Dai, let me finish the briefing, and I promise not to guild the lily or play down the danger. 'Why you', you ask? A good question when we have so many top professionals to call upon. The ISI is a well-informed security agency and will have on record details and photographs of many of our own agents. We are not sure which ones they know about, hence the need to bring in a complete outsider. A recent attempt to expose Pakistan's nuclear ambitions ended up with an SIS agent falling from a very high place without his consent or the aid of a parachute.

Since the signing of the Nuclear Proliferation treaty in 1970, another nuclear interlocutor, by the name of Anwar Husain, recently entered stage left with a big sign around his neck declaring 'If we want uranium enrichment equipment, I'm your man'.

You are familiar with the electronic aids that you will need to carry out your task. What you don't know is the location, the help and the exit strategy."

More gulps from me and a follow-up question: "Boss, do you really think I can pull this off, or am I expendable in the great scheme of things?"

No silence at all now, Hayden said: "Dai, there are some dangers, which we have sought to minimise, but we assess your chances of success at well over 80%.

Yes or no?"

My mind was in turmoil. Half of it shouted: 'Go for it!'; the other half said 'fuck off out of it and get back to the security of your family and day job'.

"OK, so where and when do I go?"

Hayden's expression did not disguise his genuine concern over his protégé's lack of confidence.

"Rightyo, here's the rest of it. The location is the Ras Koh granite hills of Changai District in the province of Baluchistan. On arrival at your destination in Pakistan, you will be monitored by one of our locals and your equipment will be already with you. Once we have finished today's business, you will be given an in-depth tutorial on how to operate it.

So, any questions?"

Dai wanted to say: 'too much information and not enough guarantees', but, instead, he elected for: "OK Boss, I'm your man but not your boy".

A wry smile spread across Hayden's face, and he nodded his appreciation. "You'll be just fine. Just keep a cool head and think of the end game.

Dai, I won't in all probability see you again. Be assured, though, that I shall follow your career with great interest. You must clear your head of all negative thoughts and trust in your innate talents, which, believe me, are up there with the best of them. As Horace once said, 'nil desperandum', or, put another way, 'never say die', Dai. So sorry, I couldn't resist it." The glint in his eye said it all. I knew Hayden had done everything within his power to safeguard my future. The rest was In'shallah.

"Thank you so much for everything you have done for me Boss. Whatever happens will be a reflection on your trust in me. I would just add that my end game was never that good."

CHAPTER 13

Exit Hayden, enter Vikram. "Hi Dai, howyadoin? Sit down, relax and make yourself comfortable, we have a long day ahead of us. I apologise for the Ladakh deception, which was orchestrated by your parent department and which, I think, could have been handled better. You saw how I used the technical equipment there. Well, here it comes again. When you see it next it will be invisible to the naked eye, the reason being that it will be built into the engine compartment of the vehicle that will take you to the Chagai hills."

"Hi Vikram, nice intro. It was good working with you in Ladakh, an experience that taught me a lot and which, I feel sure, will stand me in good stead in Pakistan. I was so worried about what happened to you and your two Sikh colleagues and can't tell you how happy I am that you all survived to tell the tale. I am less impressed, though, with the deception, as you call it, but, then again, I understand why it was done. This time around, however, I demand the truth, the whole truth and nothing but the truth.

Firstly, how do you assess my chances of success, and think carefully because I already have the assessment of my parent department?

Secondly, who will be my travelling assist in Pakistan and what is my itinerary?

And thirdly, who will be my back-up when most I need it?"

Vikram assumed a studied look and responded in measured tones: "Number 1, I have no idea what the true scale of the dangers are except to say you will have to keep your wits about you for the whole time you are in Pakistan. Number 2, you will fly to Karachi, from where you will take a connecting flight to Dalbandin from where you will be collected and taken on a long journey by car driven by a Pakistani, who is familiar with the Chagai area and who has been booked via a legitimate travel agency. He will have no idea of your real purpose and will be under the impression you are a university post-graduate who has an interest in the geographical and geological make-up of the Chagai hills -paper briefing to follow. Finally, your back-up has been hand-picked, but in all likelihood you will never meet, unless you find yourself in real difficulty. So far, so good?

Now for the bit you won't like. India has a huge interest in the outcome of your mission; London and Washington likewise. Pakistan has a pathological suspicion that my country is trying to use nuclear superiority to take control of Jammu and Kashmir – not far off the beam I have to say – and will risk anything to redress the balance.

We know they have the capability of becoming a nuclear power. What we don't know is when and how they will demonstrate it. Intelligence suggests that the moment is imminent and that they have already jumped the first few hurdles. It is your job to provide positive or negative evidence that will enable us to make informed decisions. By 'us', I mean the British government. Nothing you might discover will be disseminated to the government of India, or me for that matter. In my current capacity, I am working for HMG – he who pays the piper and all that. Do you understand?"

"Yeh, yeh Vikram, I understand. But what I am less sure about is the 'how' and the 'end game'."

"The means of detecting underground nuclear explosions by dint of seismic monitoring is nearly complete, to the point that such tests will, in the not too distant future, be identified with an accuracy of a few dozen kilometres. What we have now in the way of technical help is a piece of apparatus that has been developed in the States and which has a proven track record second to none.

What we also know is that Pakistan has already constructed a test site in Chagai District, which is situated in the extreme north west of the country, and that in all probability one or more low-key tests have already taken place there. Intelligence suggests that the preparation entailed building both vertical and horizontal shafts capable of withstanding a 20-kilotonne nuclear device exploded under one of Chagai's mountains. As you might imagine, the area is heavily protected, though by no means entirely visible to the untrained eye. Your presence within the security zone will be closely monitored, and if you make one suspicious move, they will come down on you with such ferocity you will wish you were back in your mother's womb. Understand?"

"Thanks for that, Vikram. I understand all too well, and if I had one ounce of sense inside my stupid Welsh head I would be on the next plane to Bombay.

I am a bit tired after a long day and think that I need a hot meal and a warm bed before continuing the inculcation process."

"Dai, your wish is my command, but before you retire tonight there are a few more things I have to cover for maximising your own safety.

The first is that you have to learn not just the basics of geology, but the answers to the questions that might be fired at you by belligerent and aggressive inquisitors. Your cover is paper-thin and your ability to defend it is less than robust. If you do find yourself, heaven forbid, in a situation that requires you to account for your presence in Chagai District, you have to come up with some credible answers in quick-time, like at the time of first challenge. Should you be subjected to a thorough examination of your professed knowledge, you would quickly be exposed as a fraud and, more importantly, as a spy. This has to be avoided at all costs because our ability to rescue you is not what you want to know.

Please, please read and read again your briefing on the rock formations and natural minerals of where you are going, which is rich in deposits of natural gas, coal, chromate, lead, sulphur and marble. You will, as a geologist, have with you all the accoutrements that you would need as a bona fide researcher and which you will find in your bespoke, hi-tech car, provided, naturally, by your SIS masters. Again, your written brief will tell you all you need to know. When you have read it several times, read it again and again, because it might just save your life. Then destroy it.

If you are challenged by Pakistani security forces, you must remain calm and collected at all times and assume the demeanour that only the English can muster as a fully paid-up member of a pissed-off former colonial administrator, who is being bothered unnecessarily by the local natives. It is a high-risk strategy, but most likely the only one that might get you back on the road.

OK, time to eat my friend."

I enjoyed an excellent chicken curry, which preceded yet another disturbed night's sleep. The following morning, I was woken by the usual noisy sounds of the coughs, spitting and worse of an Indian 'dawn chorus'. Breakfast was accompanied by another Vikram teaching session, the details of which were absorbed by a pupil eager to succeed. I realised, not for the first or last time, that I had not telephoned my wife to ask how she and the boys were and to say where and what I was doing. "More guilt Boyo", he thought.

On the other hand, I was genuinely worried about my decision to go to Pakistan and, just as importantly, why I had put myself in such a dangerous and avoidable situation.

'Kismet', I thought, 'Kismet.'

The rest of the morning was spent on yet more training, mainly of the geological kind, concluding with a lift to Delhi airport and an uneventful Indian Airways flight to Karachi, from where I took a less than comfortable PIA Fokker F-27 plane to Dalbandin in Baluchistan, where I was met in the tiny Arrivals hall by my driver carrying a placard paging 'Shri Dawid Richards'. David Richard's immigration clearance had already taken place in Karachi without any noticeable hitch. As it turned out, this was a somewhat over the top reception in Dalbandin as 'Dawid' was one of only six passengers on board and certainly the only one with a British name and appearance.

My driver was an extrovert fellow called Ali Khan, whose English was self-taught and comically stereotypical of a Spike Milligan or Peter Sellers character.

"Sir, Sahib, I am being here to obey your every command. Do not be forward in coming backwards and if you are needing some special favour, like a Kashmiri rug, hashish, a whore lady or a boy, you let me know. I am knowing this place so very well and am totally best person to give you what you are wanting. This is hundred percent guarantee. Also, I am having special new car given to me by my boss, who told me totally seriously that if I damage it I am probability not for walking ever again. This is saying to me that the car is definitely of the highest quality, which is all I need to know."

I was well used to this sort of patter, and simply said: "Ali my friend, all I want you to do at the moment is drive where I tell you to drive. If I need more assistance I will ask for it. Understand?"

"I am more than understanding esteemed one – I am my father's son and am here to serve your every need. Where do we go first?"

I gave Ali the directions he needed to get me to base camp one, which was located some one hundred miles or so from Dalbandin. The road was dire in every respect and required the upmost concentration from Ali, who several times seriously considered putting both hands on the steering wheel, rather than sitting side-saddle with one arm hanging limply out of the window in the manner of a Bombay taxi driver. At least he was pleased with his gleaming new car, of which he knew he had possession for just the duration of this commission.

He also was on the point of giving up all hope of finding the location from my co-ordinates in the Ras Koh hills, until, and completely randomly, he recognised his position as it loomed before his eyes against the huge landscape that unfolded before him.

CHAPTER 14

The scenery reminded me of Ladakh – bleak, barren and desolate – and filled me with utter loneliness and gut-wrenching angst, which I felt as an acute and piercing sense of anxiety or remorse.

"My god", I thought, "what have I done to deserve this hell-forsaken place?"

My professional training then kicked in and I went through the mantra of why, where, when and how. The 'why, where and when' were not in dispute, it was the 'how' that occupied my mind.

"Ali, my friend, having surveyed the area I would like you to take me a little closer to that mountain", a direction I then pointed to with my forefinger.

"And when we reach it, I would like you to park the car exactly as I say. Do you understand?"

"I am more than understanding, Sahib, just tell me when to start and stop this beautiful limo and I will do the needful and oblige. You are most important rock person and I am but a humble driver, who was put on earth to make you most important science person in Pakistan,"

"Good. That's what I like to hear. You must know that I am in a difficult part of your country for all sorts of reasons. Have you seen any signs of military presence at all and, if so, where?"

Ali's head began to move from side to side with increasing rapidity and, eventually, he managed a reply:

"Sahib, you speak words of infinitive wisdom. This is a place where local people say is training camp for Pakistan army. You know it is very remote and far beyond gaze of our Indian enemies. I am not knowing true purpose, but I think it is to keep our country safe and first-rate in world rankings."

The bespoke car having been positioned according to my instructions and Ali having been dispatched to make and drink some chai at a safe distance, I pressed some important hidden buttons within the car's interior and then took out the tools of my adopted trade. These included a tubular shaft hammer and holder, a splitting chisel and some specimen bags. As I was busying myself with the preparation process I heard the alarming noise of a vehicle approaching at high-speed, echoes of the Ladakh caper sprang to mind.

"Keep a cool head at all times", he told himself, a discipline that was to prove most challenging over the following fifteen minutes or so. What I saw was an army jeep with four soldiers aboard screeching to a halt not three feet from where I was standing. The non-driver in the front seat got out first, followed by the two men in the back.

"Vat are you doing here, I demand to know?", bellowed the leader in broken English.

"This is restricted area and you have no permit."

I did not know for certain what was subsequently said to me in Urdu, but realised that it was not friendly. Guessing, I said: "My name is David Richards, I am a post-graduate British student with an interest in the geological rock formation and mineral content of this unique part of the world. My researches are part of my PhD course, which you can check out with my university if you don't believe me."

The next thing I heard and felt was the sound and pain of a rifle butt hitting the side of my face with great force. Spitting out a couple of teeth, I uttered the words 'Ben chaud, madha chaud', which roughly translates into the pathetically over-used Americanism, 'Mother fucker' and, for good measure, includes the sister, but which in the Indian sub-Continent is universally regarded as extremely insulting and offensive. This provoked a painful, steel-capped boot into my rib cage and a concomitant feeling of nausea and not a little fear.

Whilst I was desperately trying to think of a way out of my predicament and moments before the third attack on my body took place, a second jeep arrived at the scene. After a brief conversation with his junior officer, the driver said to me in excellent English:

"My name is Captain Ismail. Apologies if my men have over-reacted, but you have to know that this part of the country has its military sensitivities. What, might I ask, are you doing here and why were we not informed officially of your presence? And, by the way, can I see your passport?"

I duly produced my passport bearing the name 'David Richards' and showing today's arrival stamp at Karachi airport. My head and ribs were aching and my brain was reeling, and I was not at all confident of being able to respond as robustly as I had been tutored. Mustering all of my inner strengths, I replied:

"I have already told your subordinate that I am a student geologist with a keen interest in the Ras Koh hills, on which I am writing a thesis and which I hope will lead to a science doctorate of philosophy from my university and not a little practical benefit to your country. You can check my credentials if you doubt me. My head and ribs hurt like hell, but I'll live if I don't get another kicking."

The Captain asked what, exactly, had brought me to Chagai District and what I expected to find here. I was well prepared for this one and trotted out the rehearsed reply, to which Ismail replied:

"That is so interesting. I too studied geology in my first year at university. My memory, though, is not so good. Can you please remind me of the two eminent British geologists who had such a profound influence on the subject in the 18th and 19th centuries?"

I reacted by saying:

"Look if you want to test my professional knowledge why don't you arrest me, throw me into a cell with some of your thugs, which I believe is a derivation of an Indian name, 'thugi' denoting base villains, and continue to beat the shit out of me? If there's one thing I can't stand is a sub-Continental pretending not to be clever."

A flicker of surprise and distaste, bordering on hatred, flashed across the Captain's eyes, but before he could react further I added:

"I think you are alluding respectively to the Englishman William Smith and the Scotsman James Hutton, the so-called fathers of English and modern geology." 'Thank you, Vikram', I thought, 'for the briefing that may have saved my life.'

This hugely risky tactic left the Captain in somewhat of a dilemma. On the one hand, his future in the Pakistan army was on the wire if he allowed a potential spy to remain at large; on the other hand, he did not want to cause a diplomatic incident that might attract unwanted attention to what he and his country were desperately trying to keep secret from the outside world.

Whilst he was trying to reconcile these two opposing thoughts, his aggressive subordinate reappeared on the scene and spoke, again in animated Urdu, which the Captain helpfully interpreted, about his interrogation of Ali, the upshot of which was that Ali had also lost a few teeth that he could hardly spare and was most definitely not part of a Western spy ring. He added that the car had been thoroughly searched and found not to contain any incriminating evidence of malfeasance.

This was sufficient for the Captain to err on the side of caution and to encourage me to conclude my geological researches, for the good of mankind, and to leave the area before sunset. With that pronouncement and after exacting sufficient data to check out my credentials, the two jeeps were gunned up and disappeared over the hill never to be seen again by either of us. We looked at one another with serious concern but a huge sense of relief.

"Sahib, I am not at all knowing what that was all about and I am wondering how I can now chew my meat having lost so many teeth.

And I have respectfully to advise you that you look worse than I feel. Is there anything I can do for you, apart from dropping my fee, which, if anything, should be increased?"

My face by now was beginning to resemble the colour of an aubergine, but my heart was singing with the possibility that I had acquired the very evidence I had been sent to capture. The proof of the pudding would have to wait another day. I busied myself for an hour or so gathering rock samples, then bagging and labelling them for future analysis by HMG nuclear scientists, who would use them to measure any evidence of nuclear activity.

The return journey to Dalbandin passed with minimal discourse, but much thought, and not a little physical discomfort by both driver and passenger. On arrival at the airport, I warmly thanked Ali for his sterling services and gave him an envelope containing more than a year's earnings accompanied with the advice that all such payments demand the promise of total silence and discretion.

"Great one, unless you have stuffed the envelope with old newspaper cuttings, I am sure you have done me a favour I don't deserve. You can rely on me one hundred percent for being three wise monkeys person. Inshallah, I hope and trust I can invite you into my humble home to meet my family when next you return to Pakistan." I said that I looked forward to accepting that kind invitation and assured him that the envelope would reveal a happy surprise.

At the same moment I noticed that the car, fingers crossed, containing the required data-capture and rock samples was being driven away by a well-dressed man who was not known to me, but who was clearly not one of Ali's colleagues.

By the time I arrived back in Delhi, I was a much changed man and not at all sure of the success or otherwise of my mission. Also, I had to come up with a credible reason for the severe bruising to my face and torso.

I took a taxi to my secret rendezvous and was met by Vikram, who did not seem in the least surprised to see my injuries, but did manage to muster a sympathetic smile and a warm welcoming hand.

"Dai, come in, make yourself comfortable and tell me all about it. I trust the other bloke looks even worse?" I tried to smile, but decided that it hurt too much.

I fell into the nearest chair and asked for alcoholic refreshment on a global scale, which appeared, as by if by magic, in double quick time. As soon as I had downed two burra pegs, my debriefing began. As is the case with such interactions, the questioner already knew some of the answers.

"Tell me, Dai, how you faired in what I know must have been a dangerous and hostile environment? Your facial, and probably other bruising would suggest that not everything went to plan. Your safe return to the mother ship suggests that you either failed heroically or succeeded magnificently. Which of the two scenarios do I report to London and what detail do I add?".

"Vikram, you are impressively perceptive and I feel sure you know far more than you are telling me. Let me be clear. My mission frightened the shit out of me and was a gnat's penis from being a complete disaster. Thankfully, your excellent briefing saved my skin and allowed me to leave Pakistan with what I think was a 'job accomplished' label.

If the car's hardware and software were fit for purpose, I think London, and doubtless Washington, will be breaking out the Bollinger big time. I could have done no more in the time available to me and in the prevailing circumstances. I absolutely do not want to repeat the experience, which I think I was so lucky to survive. Had the man with the gun decided to pull me in I would have folded like the proverbial busted flush, and the Pakistan government would have played an unbeatable hand on a world stage, thus diverting attention from whatever they might be doing contrary to any nuclear proliferation agreement.

By the way, who was the guy who drove away the car at Dalbandin airport?"

"I don't know. All I can be certain about is that he was not an agent of Pakistan's Directorate of Inter-Services Intelligence or India's Central Intelligence Bureau. The rest I leave to your imagination."

"Message received and understood."

The remaining debrief continued for another hour and consisted of the nuts and bolts information that Vikram needed to appease his masters. When there were no more questions to be asked and answered, we both heaved a sigh of relief and settled into a night's quiet celebration, which largely consisted of consuming a full litre of a famous Scottish single malt whisky. Short-term bliss in my case.

CHAPTER 15

The next morning brought with it a massive hangover and a need for a quick fix of rehydration and strong painkillers. The latter was primarily aimed at the injuries I had suffered in Chagai, the evidence of which was all too plainly seen on my face and body.

I still felt guilty about not having rung Rhiannon, who must by now have been concerned, even allowing for my poor track record in the area of family communication skills.

I decided to bite the bullet and make the call, which to my great relief was answered by our reliable housemaid, Carmen, who told me that Memsahib and the children were at Breach Candy swimming pool and were not expected back for some time. I told Carmen to be sure and tell Memsahib that I had telephoned and that I would be back in Bombay in time for dinner.

Before I left the safe house, Vikram sat me down and gave me an update on my mission. The word on the street was that I had hit the bull's eye, but that was all London was prepared to tell him. The rest would probably never follow as far as either of us was concerned. We both knew that this was the name of the game, which was predicated on the timeworn intelligence adage of 'Need to know, not nice to know'.

Emotional farewells followed and I was driven, once again, to Delhi airport for my onward journey to Bombay. I would miss my friend, Vikram.

I arrived at our apartment in the late afternoon, by which time Rhiannon and the boys had returned home.

"Good god, Dai, what do you look like? You have not been in touch for 3 days, or is it 3 weeks, and you come back looking like a you have gone 15 rounds with Cassius Clay. What have you been up to?"

My repost was almost clever:

"Sorry love, but firstly his name is now Muhammad Ali, and has been for many years, and secondly I was asked to stay on in Delhi to captain an Indian side to play a Bangladesh team at rugby, to which I said yes. Unfortunately, although we won easily, I sustained injuries to my face and body – a sure sign I must have played well. No kisses then?"

When Rhiannon saw the full impact of the injuries I had sustained in Pakistan, she was appalled and very worried that my slight frame – I was but 10 stone at the time - was not up to the rigours of the rugby code.

"Look Dai, we are going home soon. Please promise me you will not play rugby in India again. We've been married for 8 years and I would like to add another forty at least. Yes or no?"

Given the time of year and the proximity of our departure, this was not a hard one to say 'yes' to, which I duly did to Rhiannon's suspicious relief.

Farewell Dos followed in abundance and I managed to drink my way through the traumas that had preceded them without any discernible loss of self-belief and personal achievement. I had done more than I could have imagined when I left London in 1967 as a man on the brink of a nervous breakdown.

My lack of self-esteem and confidence had been replaced with a newfound belief in my ability to project myself on the wider stage, which I embraced with both arms and which I would build upon in the coming years.

I had really enjoyed my time in India, with which I felt a close affinity and for which I knew, like the mayfly, was but an ephemeral flutter of the wings of time. My short-term fame as a winning Skipper of the Bombay Gymkhana rugby team paled into all insignificance compared with what I had covertly achieved on the playing fields of Chagai District.

Final arrangements were made, mostly by Rhiannon, and we boarded a 747 Jumbo Jet for a non-stop, 8 hour flight to London Heathrow airport on 23 December 1978. Unfortunately the flight took nearly 24 hours, stopped over at Frankfurt airport - where the temperature was 5 degrees below zero - because of fog problems at

Heathrow. The fact the plane door was left open for some hours before we were allowed to disembark served only to exacerbate our younger son, Gareth's earache. In fact Gareth had not stopped crying, read 'screaming', from the time the plane first took off to the time it finally arrived at Heathrow airport, where I picked up a pre-purchased, modestly-priced car at around midnight and which I drove nearly 150 miles to Cardiff. I was so tired from the leaving-do celebrations and the dire journey from Bombay that I fell asleep at the wheel in the middle lane of a frozen M4 and was woken only because Rhiannon had remained alert in the back seat with the boys. She smacked me hard on the left shoulder and, by doing so, almost certainly saved all our lives. What an irony, I thought: "I have survived a real-time and extremely risky covert operation in a foreign country only to find myself and my family closer to the grim reaper on a drive to my home town". I pulled onto the hard shoulder and slept the sleep of exhaustion for an hour before completing the journey to Rhiannon's parents house to enjoy a very good Christmas.

CHAPTER 16

My next job in the Immigration Service was based at Adelaide House on London Bridge. The Port of London, in 1979, still attracted a large number of ships, whose foreign crews needed immigration clearance. This was not to last very long as London's merchant naval industry, and therefore its workload, was in steep decline and, within a couple of years, had virtually disappeared altogether. Visits were made in pairs, not least because getting on and off vessels carrying the tools of our trade (stamps, Suspect Index, sandwiches) in a strapped case was sometimes quite hazardous, especially when a change of tide made the gangways extremely steep and when the hospitality of the Captain had been particularly generous.

My new colleagues were an interesting collection of gifted linguists, some of whom had worked for the Secret Services during the second world war; of dedicated imbibers, some more than others; and of eccentrics, one of whom never left the office, in which he always wore his carpet slippers. Another, Alex, had fought ferociously and probably mercilessly in the killing grounds of Yugoslavia during the war and had taken a Yugoslavian bride, who, very sensibly, kept a close eye on his wallet, which he used to hide in the garage when arriving home the worse for wear, which was often and which, by the following morning, he had completely forgotten where he had placed it.

Alex was an accomplished piper and played a leading role in a London-Scottish band. His favourite saying was: "Pubs and public conveniences – never pass one, and I mean in that order!" Once, when on a Swedish ship docked at the Timber Warf and upon being offered cup of tea by the Skipper, he responded by uttering the immortal words: "Would that be Scottish tea, Captain?" Out came a bottle of Chivas Regal though still only 9am. By 10am, Alex had made considerable inroads into its contents whilst I checked around forty passports in the certain knowledge that the ship's crew were mostly squeaky clean Scandinavians.

On another momentous occasion, Alex and I found ourselves in a Soho strip club tasked with interviewing an attractive Maltese 'artiste' suspected of having conducted a marriage of convenience. Not surprisingly, the business took some time to conclude.

This was in the early days of 'after entry' work, which Adelaide House, along with the Intelligence Unit (IU) at Harmondsworth, pioneered and which was the main reason for my posting following my interesting time in Bombay. The ground-breaking IS development was inspired and advanced by an immigration officer called Geoff Vignes - the son of a Norwegian merchant sea Captain - who sadly died too soon and whose passing was mourned by a huge number of family, friends and colleagues.

Increasingly, seaman work occupied less and less of my and my colleagues' time, not least because of the continuing and accelerating dearth of ships coming to the Port of London, which by 1981 was almost moribund. Sad as this was, the emergence of a totally new dimension to UK's immigration control was exciting and challenging. I took to it like a duck to water and very soon came up with some challengingly new concepts, which, over the next two years, I honed to a point of enduring acceptance. Perhaps the most notable of my 'blue sky' ideas was to involve trustworthy employers in the development and outturn of high-level (Level 3) operations, in the process of which I managed to gain access to the companies personnel records that could and were checked against a plethora of databases. These targets included the Hilton Hotel at Hyde Park Corner, Southwark and Lambeth Councils, Shell Centre in Waterloo, Main Gas at Edmonton; and, more recently following my return to enforcement work in 1990, Saatchi & Saatchi at the time they were fronting a Tory party's electoral advertising campaign and, most sensitively, MI5's cleaning staff at Thames House, which included over 30 undesirables, about whom the less said the better, particularly, and I mean particularly, two of them. I would just add that the operation attracted the attention of the highest echelons of the Secret Service, including its head, who were most anxious to avoid any damaging publicity. The fact is that they sacked the company that they had outsourced and agreed that all future cleaners' bona fides would be checked and cleared by the immigration service. If only they had known of my own small role in the SIS they might have been even more worried. Most of the operations listed above were carried out following our office moves to Isis House and Becket House in Southwark during the eighties and nineties.

In contrast, Adelaide House's alter ego at Harmondsworth was doing some good work of its own, including a joint venture with its east London neighbour that targeted several National Car Park buildings (NCPs) in west and east London. I accompanied two of the IU's finest (Tony and Bill) to interview West African NCP staff about their immigration status. As the day unfolded after a slow start, more and more illegal immigrants filled the cells at two Met police stations in east London. Two of the staff made serious attempts to 'take off like long dogs', as Bill was to subsequently describe the events in his official report, one of whom was built like the proverbial shithouse door with shoulders like tallboys, as we say in Wales, and the other was grappled to the floor by Tony (now a very senior Home Office manager) leading to Tony breaking his watch and tearing his clothes. The written claim for compensation made interesting reading and was even short-listed for the Booker prize! The operation led to a much closer working relationship and less rivalry between the two offices, and immigration after-entry work was placed firmly on the map.

CHAPTER 17

After spending a frustrating, but useful year working on an expensive and volatile computer project at the Immigration Service's Croydon office, Lunar House, known to some as Lunatic House, I found myself back in Central London as joint manager of a large and ultimately successful enforcement office. My other half, who remains a fast friend, is an intelligent, linguistically gifted man with huge people skills and a sense of humour to match. Like me, he is now retired and, as such, represents another loss to a Service that is no longer a service, yet another tick in the dead dinosaurs box by the new brooms with their new world management speak as they sweep their way aimlessly to an unreachable goal.

Apropos nothing at all, I recall an embarrassing event that took place during that period in my life, when I was staying temporarily with an Indian friend of mine in New Malden. I had arranged to be interviewed by a very bright Oxford university student, who was writing a dissertation on immigration related matters and who was the daughter of another Indian friend from the same neck of the London woods. I had foolishly agreed to see her at my friend's house far, far too early, given my friend's generosity of spirit – and I use the term literally – on the occasion of the previous evening. From deep slumber, I just about heard the door bell ringing and just about stopped myself opening the door whilst still stark naked. An alarmingly hasty apology for not being quite ready, a frantic search for my clothes, not all put on in the right order, I managed at last to lift the latch. There, standing on the doorstep, was this very attractive, bright-eyed and bushy-tailed young lady, notepad and pen in hand, awaiting an invitation to come in.

"Hello, my name's Samira Ahmed – my father, whom you know, asked if you would be kind enough to answer a few questions (read two hours' worth) about your speciality subject. I hope this is not a bad time to arrive? (read, what do you look like?)"

Having sat her down, made a seriously strong cup of coffee for me and poured a glass of water for her, I made a huge effort to plug into some of my much-reduced mental faculties to a point that (almost) enabled intelligent intercourse. Her line of questioning was worryingly incisive and went far beyond the average knowledge of an inquisitive undergraduate. When she left, apparently satisfied with her Q&A, I went straight back to bed in a state of utter exhaustion.

Samira is now a regular contributor to Channel 4 News, which she sometimes fronts when, John Snow, otherwise known as - don't look at-my-tie-which-I-and-the-equally-in-denial-Mr Paxman- do not think-we-should-be-wearing- is away. I like to think my carefully prepared tutorial helped her on her way. But I suspect she would have made it anyway!

I was to experience many other memorable chapters in my chosen career before my retirement in 2006, but none as satisfying as my role in the field of immigration intelligence.

A bit of nifty footwork next saw me as the manager of a regional Intelligence unit in 2002, a position for which I had a real feel, some even said flair, though my natural modesty prevents me from acknowledging that, as all my friends would testify! This unit was seen as a template for others to emulate in a Service that did not and still does not universally embrace the concept of necessary and essential intelligence work.

We majored in providing operational staff with blue-chip intelligence on a raft of immigration-related topics, ranging from profiles and methodologies of abusive asylum seekers and their facilitators, to named suspect individuals and vehicles, to upstream disruption of organised criminal gangs in provider countries, such as Turkey and Greece, to combating the harm factors associated with human trafficking and to complying with emerging best practice such as the National Intelligence Model. The unit boasted the best team of immigration intelligence Analysts in the country as well as very productive working relationships with immigration colleagues and stakeholders in France, Belgium, The Netherlands, Italy, Germany, Turkey, Greece, Malta, Cyprus and many of the new eastern European EU States. My local support was magnificent, with just a few exceptions, and was particularly bolstered with people with a real feel for their chosen work. As they say, no names, no pack drill. But they know who they are.

That said, one of my most able lieutenants, nay my most able lieutenant, was a lady who was born to intelligence work, for which she had an innate, inventive and innovative gift. Ursula (pseudonym, of course) could look at a set of apparently unrelated events and, somehow, link them together without the aid of limitless resources. An example of this gift was when I and my boss were guests of the local police chiefs, who were hosting a visit of the then home secretary. Minutes before the Secretary of State's entry to the assembled audience, I received a telephone call from Ursula, who advised me that we were about to be invaded by huge numbers of eastern European gypsies and should I not advise said home secretary of this intelligence before it became a national embarrassment. This was a particularly difficult call for me to make, given my lack of immediate access to the relevant data and the fact I was about to be surrounded by the Chief Constable and a raft of his senior managers. I was aware of the increasing arrivals of Roma hopefuls, mainly from Slovakia and the Czech Republic, but not of the scale of the problem.

I put my trust, as usual, in Ursula's sound judgement and advised Mr Blunkett that he should take appropriate counter-measures with no time to lose. He was seriously annoyed that this intelligence had come to him in the forum he found himself in (ie unprepared), but rose to the situation by demanding that senior immigration officials, far above my pay-scale, take immediate action to visit the source countries and 'STOP IT!'. Not bad, I thought, for an off-the-cuff intervention, at the same time thinking that my gut reaction could go horribly wrong. As it turned out, Ursula had got it exactly right, thanks to a most talented Analyst in my team. The avalanche began within weeks, with the arrival of thousands of gypsies claiming asylum in the UK – a haemorrhage that was staunched only because of the swift pressure applied to the then two EU aspirant countries on the basis of intelligence provided. Top marks to Ursula and particularly to the Analyst who had made the required intelligence connections and who went on to provide much appreciated professional support to the senior delegations to the source countries.

This represents but one example of the team's major successes over a five year period. There were many, many more involving intelligence officers and their managers than I am able to refer to. Suffice to say that individuals within the various bespoke teams took affirmative action against a raft of organised immigration-related criminals and their criminality across many international borders, largely without their operational colleagues' knowledge or appreciation. Such is life.

My background in pre, on and after entry immigration work enabled me to make informed decisions on how best to 'sell the product' to both senior managers and frontline troops. Having an excellent team of professionals working to me made the task all the easier, but it was one that you could never turn your back on for fear of sniper fire from the uninitiated and the never-wasers.

As with all of my former team, she and they must remain nameless, but I cannot leave this page without mentioning my gratitude to them (with a few exceptions) for the mostly unrecognised response by peers and senior management to their many top quality products.

During this period of my career I was to receive one more invitation to serve my country in a non-immigration role.

Prior to this, however, Rhiannon had given birth to two beautiful daughters, Elizabeth and Natalie, both of whom were to do well at school and university. Meanwhile the 'boys' were to become good musicians in Sussex and in London, the older as a guitarist and songwriter and the younger as an accomplished drummer and tour manager.

Unfortunately, not one of them could play chess to save their lives. Hey ho, my fault I suppose.

CHAPTER 18

So, life remained good, and whilst I had considerably slowed down in my late fifties, I was to be given one last opportunity of contributing to the 'Security of the State'. No more soft approaches from Hayden, whose obit had, some years earlier, appeared in several broadsheets, albeit suitably sanitised. Sadly missed and much mourned.

My security clearance remained at Developed Vetting (DV) level, which allowed me into the inner sanctum of SIS' green and cream headquarters at Vauxhall Cross, which I had been invited to attend one sunny day in late July 2004, just 2 years and a bit before my retirement.

My interlocutor was a well-dressed man in his early thirties – clearly, I surmised, an Oxbridge graduate and clearly already well up the greasy pole. His manner was polite enough, but I detected a hard edge, which was in direct contrast with that of Hayden, who was the very epitome of urbane charm and consummate under statement. My own Service had been infiltrated by senior officers from other government departments, most notably, some would say detrimentally, by managers from the Prison Service and HM Customs & Excise, not many of whom had or have a clue on how the Service should be run let alone how to manage staff who did or do. What a bloody shame. UKIS RIP.

"May I call you Dai or would you prefer a more formal relationship? My name, by the by, is Justin and my speciality lies in the Middle East."

"Would that be Bow or Bethnal Green?" I ventured to ask, keeping as straight a face as I could muster. And, please, by all means call me Mr Morgan."

This did nothing for raising the room temperature in what was fast becoming a very chilly atmosphere or for removing the rictus grin and fiercely cold eyes on Justin's face.

"OK, let no-one accuse me of having had a sense of humour bypass. Before getting to the nitty-gritty of why you are here today, can I ask you if you, at your advanced age, are up for a final mission, subject, of course, to how you view the risk factors? In broad outline, it involves a journey to Iran. Your personal file tells me you have been just about everywhere else in the world in search of the Holy Grail or something resembling it." A quick look at Dai to see if his joke had found favour. To his chagrin, there was no response.

" Justin, sorry, I don't know your surname, there is as much chance of me going to Iran than you being invited to the Edinburgh Festival as a stand-up comedian. The Indian sub Continent, though not without its dangers, was at least known to me in terms of culture and politics. I have no idea of either discipline in Iran, which I am as interested in visiting as going to Siberia in the depths of winter with no clothes on, if you follow my drift."

"What a shame, Mr Morgan – my name is Smith if you want to know – only do me one favour. Can I escort you to another room to speak with someone with whom you are acquainted? If you then remain as adamantly opposed to what is on offer, that will be fine. If you change your mind, I shall still be here to take you through next steps."

He took me down the corridor and into a smaller room, in which there was a coffee table and four easy chairs. He left me alone for a minute or two, following which a side door opened, through which my good friend Vikram appeared.

"My god, Vikram, what on earth are you doing here?", realising as I said it that I knew all too well what he was doing here.

"Daijee Sahib, I am being flown into London to make you incredible offer of great fame and forever star person. All you do is sign on the line of best contract and you will never after feel any pain. And my final pension will be increased beyond my wildest expectation."

"Hey, Vikram, why are you acting like a fucking chichi and why haven't you got the whisky out?"

"Goddamit, my good friend, it's good to see you again after all these years. I hear you continue to increase the Morgan clan to try and compete with the UK's nonindigenous population, but forget it Pal, we will win hands down. Why, because we Indians are the phallic champions of the world."

"Sounds like a challenge to me, Vikram. And by the way, are you saying that bald men are more potent than those of us with a full head of non-dyed hair?"

Vikram had indeed aged beyond his years. He was roughly my age, but looked considerably older, and I wondered why.

"Vikram, how has life treated you since we last met in Delhi all those years ago? You were then a young man, as I was, now we are both much older and probably not a lot wiser."

"I have, like you, been blessed with a good marriage, four children and a double career that has been a challenge, I have to say. My own organisation has been good to me and yours has provided me with the financial rewards not available to me in India. I would add that I have never compromised the security of my country, which has benefited significantly from my double agent role. The SIS need one more push from you, doubtless your man will fill in the detail, and just as certain is the reason they went to the expense of bringing me here.

They anticipated a negative response, who wouldn't, and took out the insurance associated with true friendship. Quite clever when you think about it.

I, like you, am not far off retirement age, and the carrot offered is to ensure that I and my family will benefit from a positive result today. That said, Dai, I would no more trick you into accepting an impossible assignment than kill myself, my wife and my children. I have spent the last 4 days immersed in what I believe to be a totally worthwhile and doable project, provided you decide to accept it. The dangers, though, are very real, more so than those you were exposed to in Pakistan.

Iran, as you know, is not known to possess Weapons of Mass Destruction and has signed treaties repudiating holding them. What we don't know for certain is what their current and future intentions are, given the belligerent stance they are taking on the world stage.

In 1979 the monarchy was replaced by the Islamic Republic. Iran's nuclear progamme began in the Shah's era, including a plan to build 20 nuclear reactors. Following the revolution in 1979, all nuclear activity was suspended. Current plans extend to the construction of 15 power reactors and 2 research reactors. It is evident that Iran's efforts are focused both on uranium enrichment and a parallel plutonium effort. It claims it is trying to establish a complete nuclear fuel cycle to support a civilian energy programme, but this same fuel cycle would equally apply to a nuclear weapons development programme. Not only that, Iran appears to have spread its nuclear activities over a number of sites to reduce the risk of detection or attack.

By later this year, as close as that, Iran could be producing fissile material for atomic bombs using both uranium enrichment at Natanz and plutonium produced at Arak. I could say more, but I think you might want to say something first."

"What a good chap you are, Vikram, and never one to over egg the cake. Without compromising your brief, can I ask you to tell me in laymen's terms what I am being asked to do that no-one else in this bespoke organisation can do?"

"The exact terms of your mission, of which I am understandably out of the loop, will be explained to you by your SIS colleagues. My advice though, for what it's worth, is to give the offered terms your close attention and to err on the side of acceptance. I say this, Dai, because I know from past experience that there is no-one better qualified to cut the mustard on this one. I remain a trusted friend and I will be in London until tomorrow evening should you wish to buy me an expensive lunch in celebration of a momentous occasion."

"Vikram, whatever I decide, the lunch is on me. We have a lot to catch up on and I need to probe your mind to the point that your brain hurts."

"Sounds good to me, you can find me at the Dorchester Hotel. I shall await your call and your final decision."

With that someone somewhere pressed a button, heralding Justin's return to the scene and my return to his room.

"Mr Morgan, I do hope your little chat with Vikram was helpful and constructive. You will have gathered that he is not aware of the full extent of the mission, of which I shall speak more should you wish to proceed to the next level. Yes?"

"Mr Smith, I am ready to proceed to next steps, but remain firmly opposed to jumping from pan to fire. Whatever is on offer has to be blue-chip or better. Know what I mean?"

"Understood. I have the necessary detail, which I hope will bring you on side?"

The 'necessary detail' came as somewhat of a surprise. No state of the art motor with in-built nuclear explosion detectors; no geologist cover; and no quick in and out.

"Mr Morgan (with the emphasis on 'Mr'), Iran is not known to possess Weapons of Mass Destruction (WMD) and has signed treaties repudiating possession of them" ('same brief as Vikram's, I surmised'). "The US national intelligence judged that Iran halted an active nuclear weapons programme in 2003 and that it remained the case until now. It also estimates that Iran is technically capable of producing enough highly enriched uranium for a weapon sometime between 2010 and 2015.

Just 2 months ago former Deputy Commander-in Chief of British Land Forces, General Sir Hugh Beach, along with former Cabinet ministers, scientists and campaigners joined a delegation to Downing Street opposing military intervention in Iran. The delegation delivered two letters to Tony Blair from 1800 physicists warning that military intervention and the use of nuclear weapons would have disastrous consequences for the security of Britain and the rest of the world. Added to which, the House of Commons, only last week, challenged the PM's statement that Iran and Syria are to blame for the latest crisis in the Middle East. And I don't mean east London."

"So why the concern if everything is as hunky-dory as you say?"

"Both the US and Israel are convinced that the proliferation hiatus in Iran is but a temporary situation. Israel, in particular, has not ruled out a strike similar to the one they carried out on an Iraqi nuclear plant at Osirak in 1981.

The British position is not dissimilar, but, as I have outlined, there are difficulties in us taking a hawkish stance. That is not to say that we should sit on the fence. No, no, quite the contrary, but we do need to adopt the tortoise rather than the hare route to achieve the result that we in the West want."

"Mr Smith (with the emphasis on the 'Smith'), this is all very interesting, but what do you envisage my role to be in the great scheme of things?"

" Ah yes, therein lies the rub. What we crave is for someone with an aptitude of playing very good chess to enter a Master's tournament in Tehran and, between games, to turn a certain Iranian scientist with the offer of a big slice of London's golden pavements. This is no ordinary Iranian scientist – he is a major force in his country's nuclear development and is known to be an expert in nuclear fission."

"Look, you talked about getting down to the nitty-gritty, assuming the term is not a hanging offence in the current PC handbook. I have not played competitive chess for forty five years and would be seen as a joke at an international event, notwithstanding a dearth of Grand Masters. Secondly, I know from my dealings with my SIS recruiter that you have on your books much better chess players than I ever was or could have been. So why me?"

"You talk of ancient history. In the best part of three decades since you last spoke to Hayden, the Firm has lost and not replaced its expert chessmen. You are the only one left. The **only** one. Our target in Tehran is a very keen, but not a top-flight player whose entry into the competition was agreed only because he represents the host nation. Unfortunately, there is no way we can recruit and train someone else in the time frame available to us. We assume your talent for the game remains only dormant and that a crash restoration course would get you to the point that you would not bring you to the attention of the Iranian thought police. That premise has to be a given."

I started to think the impossible. Could I get my chess skills back to where they were when I was fifteen and did I want to push my luck one last time? And what the fuck was I supposed to do with an Iranian nuclear scientist who just happened to like playing chess?

"OK Justin, let's start to get friendly. Accepting that I could raise my chess game to the required level, and that's big if, how on earth do I 'turn' a man so essential to the Iranian nuclear cause?"

"Dai, the board game is a given, for which arrangements are already in place, and the target is half way there, as will be explained at your formal briefing, should you accept the mission.

The time scale is from 13 to 19 August, which will enable you to fly to Tehran in an identity to be chosen, compete in the chess tournament, carry out your tasking and return to the UK in time for you to attend a BBQ we know you have been invited to. You will need to book a week's annual leave, but tell your nearest and dearest, but no-one else, that you have to make an urgent visit to Turkey to discuss developments in a major intelligence operation you are embroiled in. It will come as no surprise to her.

And before you ask, your name has come out of the hat because you are not known to anyone in the Middle East and because, to be brutally honest – a rare thing in my business – you would not be linked with our organisation no matter what checks were made were your mission to be compromised".

"You mean if things go tits up?", I asked.

"I cannot deny there is a risk or that our man will play ball when he is faced with a life-changing decision, but our best brains think there will be a positive outcome provided the wheels do not come off in unforeseen circumstances. Yes or no?"

I sat there for what seemed an eternity, but in reality was probably no more than a few seconds.

" OK Justin, you silvery tongued bastard, I'm your man, but I have to tell you that whatever anatomical part of my body can be crossed is crossed. Also, I want a good wedge in my or my family's hand whether or not I get back to Blighty. Agreed?"

"Agreed, Dai. The exact terms, including tax and NI deductions, will be made available to you and you will not be disappointed. Hopefully.

A full briefing will be given to you before you embark on this important project. We shall be in touch. And good luck" (In parenthesis, 'you'll need it').

The next day and after dossing down at the Civil Service Club, I had lunch with Vikram at a very good north London Punjabi restaurant just off the Tottenham Court Road that I had frequented many years ago.

I arrived in time to speak to the patron and to impress upon him that my guest was a Michelin Guide scout who specialised in Indian cuisine and whose opinion was globally valued. It was imperative, though, that the house did not give any indication of its knowledge of this fact, but, rather, behaved as naturally as possible. When asked why I had given them the heads up, I simply replied (read 'lied through my teeth') that I had, many years ago, experienced the most romantic evening of my life at this restaurant and that this tip-off was by way of pay-back.

Enough said. The table was chosen and the scene set. Vikram arrived on time and we both sat down to an aperitif.

" My friend", I said, " this is your day, which I want you, as my guest, to enjoy so much that you might think of coming back again."

"Dai, let's see where the afternoon takes us. And let's not forget why I am here".

"Accha tikai, in pursuit of that goal, what's your poison?"

We settled for something hugely liver-damaging and then proceeded to work our way through a meal fit for the gods, Vikram being a most honoured and valued recipient. By the time Vikram had to leave to pack and catch his plane, we had sorted out most of the world's problems.

I saw Vikram to his hotel, assured him of my undying respect and told him that we should get together, family to family, before he lost even more hair.

CHAPTER 19

The next 3 weeks were hell. Any thought of getting back to the heady days of my chess youth soon evaporated. I read all the right the books on openings and end games, reminded myself about the great World Champions of yore and played a myriad of games against a high-level computer software program, which beat me with monotonous and humiliating regularity. I beefed up on my chess knowledge of the Greats, which largely centred on the likes of Emanuel Lasker, the romantic and charismatic José Raúl Casablanca, Alexander Alekeine - arguably the greatest of them all – the wonderful Mikhail Botvinik, if I leave the brilliant Tal out it is at my peril, and, more recently, the gifted but hugely disturbed Bobby Fisher, who, in July 1972, globally turned upside down the domination of the Russians by beating Boris Spassky in Reykjavik ; and, finally, the world champion chess genius between 1985 and 1993, Gary Kasparov. Huge respect, I have to say. However, I did not return to the games of a man who held the title for a decade between 1975 and 1985, Anatoly Karpov, because, talented player that he was, rightly or wrongly, he was held to be a pawn (pun definitely intended) and mouthpiece of the corrupt and fast disintegrating Soviet empire.

A bit of history for those of you with an interest. In 1914, Nicholas II, Czar of all the Russias, hosted a legendry chess tournament, to which he personally donated one thousand roubles towards the prize money. The reigning world champion was Emanual Lasker, who had not played competitive chess for five years.

Most of the world's top players took part, including José Raúl Casablanca, who was, at the time, a brilliant and up-and-coming Cuban super star. Akibi Rubinstein was also there and was arguably the most in-form player of the day, having won five tournaments on the trot. Many other great players made up the cast on what became a stage of high drama, which, in its final moments, reminded me, at a much lesser level in my humble case, of the appearance of confidence against the reality of no confidence whatsoever.

Lasker called chess 'a fight'; Boris Spassky referred to it as 'a sport'; and others have claimed it to be a science or an art. The fact is that all these qualities are present. Reuben Fine, one of the world's great players and a gifted psychologist, wrote in a chess treatise that 'a combination of homosexual and hostile elements are sublimated in chess.' He went on to say that the King on the chessboard is indispensable, all important, irreplaceable, yet weak and requiring protection. The King therefore symbolises a boy's penis in the phallic stage, with the attendant castration complex. What bollocks!!

Capablanca led until the eighteenth out of twenty one rounds and lost to Lasker by not converting pressure into points and by losing a winning position against Tarrasch in the next game. Lasker went on to win the tournament by one half of a point, with Alekhine snatching third position.

At the conclusion of events, the Czar coined the phrase 'Grand-master of chess', which munificence was bestowed upon the top five competitors.

A momentous occasion for the game, but an earth-shattering disappointment for Capablanca, who was devastated by 'bottling' a great chance to beat the world champion in a fair fight. Unlike unlucky Paul Keres, he at least went on to win the world championship.

I had forgotten how talented these players were and how difficult it was to follow the multi-faceted logic and three-dimensional workings of their minds. The Welsh chess motto is: 'attack is the best form of defence'. The central theme to attacking dominance is, indeed, 'central'. The middle four squares on the chessboard control everything – the other sixty squares are merely the killing ground. For those of you not familiar with the primary purpose of the game, winning can be achieved either by a total avalanche of pressure or, much less frequently, the toppling of your opponent's King by means of checkmate. This occurs when said King is unable to escape from a losing position, is utterly defeated and falls to the ground, usually with the help of the index finger. Controlling those four squares does not necessarily mean occupying them. More importantly, it focuses on deploying your pieces in such a way that your opponent's battalions are under threat and that he is spending more time defending his King and other big hitters than he is on launching an attack of his own. An example of this is the move known as 'fiancetto' (from the Italian word meaning 'engagement'), which places the bishop on the second row directly in front of the knight with the knight's pawn just one square ahead of him. If both bishops are so mobilised, they act rather like long-range snipers, whose sights are aimed diagonally and cover all four central squares. I say 'he', but I always found it ironic that, in a largely male dominated game, the strongest piece on the board is the Queen, who can move in any direction provided there is not another piece in her way. Not much change there, then.

When, from the age of thirteen to fifteen, competing as a member of my County senior team and sat opposite one of the many 'old' men I was pitted against – at least, they seemed old - smoking a pipe or worse, I found it very difficult to concentrate on the board, usually because I could hardly see it because it was enveloped in smoke. Also, the smell of my opponent and his habit (nearly everyone smoked at the time) was extremely off-putting to the delicate nostrils of a relatively young boy. I cannot remember exactly how many games I won, drew or lost, but I know I won far more than I lost, which did not please the 'old' buggers at all.

I was reminded, however, of my own shortcomings and of the 'nearly waser' status (again, with apologies to John Le Carré) that summed up my own feeble attempts towards stardom in the 1960s. I studied and studied in the certain knowledge that I was fighting against the tide of time. After a couple of weeks I felt I had done enough to busk it provided I maintained a cool head. The more I thought about it the more I convinced myself that this would prove to be a high-risk, and probably no-win, venture.

My chess preparations continued with some limited help from my SIS masters. What they did far more usefully for me was to inculcate me into the relevant details of the Iranian terrain, politics, risk factors, players and the latest update on their nuclear aspirations.

As for my target, I attended three long sessions on how he operated on a psychological, metaphysical, chess, family, job, political and logical level, following which I still did not have a clue as to who he really was.

Karim Alijani, was an accomplished nuclear scientist – assisted by a 3 year course at a top London university - for which read 'spy infiltrator' of whom there was an abundance in the 1980s - and enjoyed many of the so called weaknesses of the human condition, doubtless kindled by the delights of the flesh pots of Soho and the like. He was brilliant in his field and he knew it, and was seen by western powers as a huge prize were he to be 'brought over'.

CHAPTER 20

Homework done, legend in place and visa and other logistics sorted, I flew to Tehran in the name of David Craig-Marshall, who was a minor British chess Master and who would be totally out of contact for some weeks to come. In fact, longer than that because he did not actually exist. The legend built around the identity, they said, was absolutely watertight, no matter how deeply it was probed.

I booked into my hotel, the venue of the tournament, unpacked my case and waited for a call on my secure mobile phone. Nothing. The chess tourney would commence the following day and I had to convince myself that I could cut the mustard both as a chess player and as a spy.

Now 8pm and still no contact. What the fuck was going wrong. I ate a light meal and, to keep my mind active, read up on a few chess openings. 9pm and still no contact. Worried or what? An hour later I was fast asleep and dreaming of images more associated with Dante's Inferno than the serene world of an international chess tournament.

"What's that noise on the radio, getting louder by the second? No, wait a minute, it's not on the radio, it's on my phone. Christ, my phone and I'm not answering it".

I shot out of bed, picked up the mobile, pressed the receive button and waited for a voice I was hoping to hear.

"Hi, is that Mr Craig-Marshall? My name's Grant Williams and I am making contact much later than I had planned to, for which my sincerest apologies. As you know I am your travel guide in Tehran and, as such, I want to make your time here as pleasant as possible. The reason for my late call is hugely domestic and I hope you won't ask me now for too much detail. I'm in the lobby should you feel able to join me."

My heart jumped longer than Lyn the Leap in his hay day and my instinct was to do a bit of local surveillance before committing myself to a full frontal, hail fellow well met. I dressed, and as in the best 007 books, left a hair and a 'Do not disturb' card on my room door that would tell me if anyone had entered my room in my absence, and I then proceeded to the balcony overlooking the lobby. There he was, my man, sipping a drink of something or another and with no visible sign of a minder. I waited for another few minutes before nonchalantly moving in.

"Mr Williams, I presume", and in hushed tones, "Vikram you nutter . Number one, why are you here as my back-up and number two why are you so late?"

"Hello Dai, so sorry to ring you at this hour. My flight from Delhi arrived in Tehran 5 hours late and my orders were not to contact you over the phone from abroad. Anyway, I'm here now and very much in an assist role.

Before we go any further, can I invite you to enjoy a coffee with me at a nearby café, at the same time pointing to the walls and then to his mouth and ears. I nodded my understanding and we repaired to said café, which was just a short walk from the hotel.

Once we were seated at a suitable table Vikram said:

"The local SIS chief is, as you will know, aware of your presence but does not know the detail. I shall remain for the duration of your mission and will feed you with developments elsewhere as they occur. If you need emergency help, I shall do my best to provide it, but be aware that this country is as volatile as a swarm of killer bees awaiting orders to strike. Not sure what you have been told in London about your target, Karim Alijani, but you might find a bit of Indiacraft will help."

"Vikram, any help from you would be gratefully received. I have to tell you that I am not at all optimistic about my chances of success. This country is as foreign to me as foreign gets; the chess tournament is a complete lottery; and the target is a total and unpredictable enigma. I am no longer sure why I accepted the job, despite your kind words of assurance. Please, what can you add to the pot?"

"OK, your man is half way to crossing the line, but, and this is big but, he has a lot of close family members who will not be able to leave Iran. The potential for emotional blackmail is large. You will have no influence over their destinies and you must, under no circumstances, unduly factor them into your game plan. I cannot overstate the importance of getting Karim to the place he craves and belongs, but equally, I cannot overstate the difficulties in achieving this."

"What else can you tell me that will 'assist' me along the road?"

"Dai, tomorrow, as you know, is a day of registration and briefings in the morning, so no immediate worries about playing the game after lunch. There is a real and likely threat from the mullahs' Ministry of Intelligence (MOI) - also referred to as VEVAK – which are the current names of the Iranian secret service. It was previously known as

SAVAMA and, before that, as SAVAK. But you will know all of this from your London briefings.

President Mahmoud Ahmadinejad, as you know, calls the shots and would not be at all impressed if his top nuclear physicist skipped the country to join forces   with the west. The head of the Ministry of Intelligence since August 2005 is one Gholan Hossein Mohseni-Ejehei. Don't look to him to give you a helping hand. By the way, I'm staying just down the corridor from you, room 509.

What additional intelligence you need to know about our friend, Karim is off-CV but focus on his life-style and personal preferences, information known to my organisation, though not necessarily to yours.

He is a good family man – wife and two children – but has a penchant for men friends of the 'other' persuasion. A bit like Oscar Wilde but not as witty. What he is good at is making nuclear bombs from their constituent parts, most of which are already available to him at this moment in time.

What you need to do, once you have made tournament contact, is speak to him one-to-one and convince him into agreeing to an exit strategy that safeguards his and his family's interests. You will know how much money you have at your disposal and how you might effect his defection, but perhaps what you might not know is that he is already under scrutiny by the MOI because of his exploitable sexual weakness. That means he is under constant surveillance, which, in turn, means that anyone talking to him will be closely picked-over and that all conversations with him could be monitored and recorded."

"Thanks, Vikram, as usual you have provided me with the missing pieces from what I believe to be an extremely complex jig-saw puzzle. See you at breakfast, say 0730hrs?"

"Fine. Sleep well."

CHAPTER 21

I did indeed sleep well, more from exhaustion than a clear mind. Following a brief breakfast with Vikram, whose cover for knowing me was well rehearsed, I toddled along to the main conference room, which was large and already half-full of players and administrators, not to mention two or three leather-jacketed men who stood adjacent to the man I recognised from photographs as Karim Alijani.

So, the stage was set. How it would play out was anyone's guess, but I would give it my best shot. It took a hour or so to register my presence, produce my passport (which I had to temporarily retrieve from the Reception desk on the promise of return immediately it was no longer required for chess purposes) and identify who I was drawn against that afternoon. It was a Swedish Master, unusually called Johansson, who was not known to me, which, hopefully, was a good sign that he was not top notch.

There followed a tourny talk from the representative form FIDE, the world chess organisation that had united, in 2006, with Gary Kasparov's break-away group after a turbulent period of personality clashes. A rather less interesting briefing was then given by an Iranian official with limited English, absolutely no sense of humour and an assignment to scare us shitless were we foolish enough to breach the letter or the spirit of Islamic law and/or culture.

The contenders for what was a modest amount of money and a rather gaudy trophy numbered 32 players from 16 countries, most of whom seemed to know one another. I was approached by a Belgian and a Swiss, who introduced themselves and asked if I was the new kid on the block. I replied that, at an age of nearly 60, I could hardly lay claim to that title. To save them, or anyone else, further curiosity, I added that I had attained Master's accreditation when I was much younger, but had remained out of formal competition for the last twenty plus years. I noted the look on their faces of relief based on the certain knowledge that I was not a serious contender. So far, so good.

After lunch, I sat down at a competition chess table for the first time in 45 years and inwardly prayed for an acceptable outcome. I had the black pieces and played a conservative French Defence, which I knew from my youth was heading for a draw from move one. Fortunately, Mr Johansson went along with my theory and, after 35 moves, offered me the draw, which I gratefully accepted.

Between moves I spotted where Karim was playing and noted that he was looking somewhat worried – not surprising since he was playing the top seed, a Russian who had once, not long ago, been a Grand Master. Shortly after my dismal draw, I saw Karim gently toppling his King in dispirited surrender. His bodyguards decided that this was a good time to take a break, which allowed me the opportunity to sidle over, introduce myself and offer some feeble words of consolation. He studied me for longer than I felt comfortable with and said:

"Please, Mr Craig-Marshall, you are very kind. I was never in the game and he is such a strong player that I will be amazed if he does not win the tournament without losing a match."

"Please call me David. I fear, looking at the form book, that you are correct in your assumption and I do not look forward to pitting my wits against him any time soon. As we have finished relatively quickly, perhaps we can have a few games of lightning chess before dinner?".

"Of course, I would enjoy that, and, who knows, it might sharpen both of us up for tomorrow".

We reassembled the board and proceeded to move the chessmen around at a speed of no more than 5 seconds at a time. I was always pretty good at this version of the game and found that my touch had not altogether deserted me. Over the next hour, we played five or six games, nearly all of which went in my favour.

"David, you play very well and with lots of panache and guile. Perhaps we can meet up tonight or, at least, before the end of the competition for another session. I would like that."

"Karim, if I may call you by your first name, I too would like that. I have a commitment this evening, but am free tomorrow night if that suits you. I have to say, though, that I have observed your entourage and would prefer not to see you in their company, if you know what I mean."

"Of course. They are course fellows sent to keep an eye on me for security reasons. I shall tell them that I am not well and am having an early night. You can come to my room, 741, at, say 8pm and we can play for a couple of hours if that's OK with you".

The opening moves were complete and we were now moving into the middle game, which was always my forte. I spent the next few hours wandering about Tehran pretending I was a tourist.

I visited the old royal quarter, which has all but vanished except for the Golestan Palace and gardens, which was one of the residences of the Qajar kings and also houses the famous 'Hall of Mirrors'. I managed to get to the Azadi (Freedom) Tower, which includes a cultural centre with a library, a museum and art galleries displaying works by contemporary artists. The tower was designed by a young Iranian architect, was finished in 1971, stands 45 metres high and comprises an impressive large central block on four splayed feet. It acts as a grandiose gateway to the capital. There was more to be seen, but not on that occasion. I apologise if I am beginning to sound like a tourist guide, which strikes fear into my very soul.

I returned to my hotel, or, rather, the small coffee shop very near to the hotel, and met up with Vikram, as planned.

" Not a bad result, Dai. I've bet five rupees you will not be last come Friday."

"That's very reassuring, Vikram, considering there are in excess of 60 rupees to the pound. Did you cop my meeting with the target?".

'Oh yes, and very neat too. I think he's got the 'hots' for you, so keep your back to the wall and don't do your shoe laces up unless he's at least 10 yards away and fully dressed."

"You're so course. Stop arsing about and tell me what, if anything, you've discovered today."

"OK. The leather jackets are low life VEVAK soldiers, who rotate around the clock to keep an eye on our man. Surveillance suggests that their hearts are not in the job, as, frequently they take a communal break, sometimes for over an hour, to do whatever they do. I'll be in a better position tomorrow to provide you with likely times that might offer themselves up for a one-to-one."

" I've already arranged to meet Karim in his room - don't even think it - at 8pm tomorrow. You will have to let me know if this is likely to be a bad time for an unchaperoned meet. Also, I might have to move quickly before the end of the tournament if I deem it appropriate. The exit strategy is complicated and involves a third country and a lot of hard travelling. And when I say 'hard' I mean really hard."

Vikram assumed a look of genuine concern, but did not ask any questions. We parted and did not see one another for dinner in order not to attract too much attention to our all too visible relationship. I joined the Belgian and Swiss contenders' table, ate an average, alcohol-free meal and returned to my room for an early night, which I sorely needed.

CHAPTER 22

Tuesday was another early start. Having washed, dressed and breakfasted, I made for the Conference room whilst it was relatively quiet. I noted my next opponent was a German whose name was vaguely familiar, and who, on checking my records, I saw was at the top end of the Masters points range, having won two recent tournaments that had put him within striking distance of gaining Grand Master status. My afternoon opponent was the Belgian I had met earlier.

I shook hands, sat down and started the clock. It was my turn to have the white pieces, which afforded me the opportunity of playing my favourite Queenside opening. The game moved on for an hour or so and I felt a distinct feeling of resignation -not a word we chess players like to use lightly- that told me of my impending annihilation. He was out-manoeuvring me big-time and did not appear to be breaking sweat. Just as things were about to reach a denouement, I noticed that, in his arrogance, he had committed the Cardinal sin of not guarding his King, so hell-bent was he on toppling mine. Worse than that, there was no escape for him, meaning that in four moves I would checkmate him.

I looked at him and he looked at me, disdainfully I have to say, and very slowly moved his right index finger towards his monarch, which fell over, almost in slow-motion, much to the amazement of all within viewing distance. He raised himself imperiously from his chair and said to me: "Both you and I know that this should never have happened. I had you beaten all ends up and, by dint of shear luck and no talent, you found yourself in a winning position."

"I agree, Sir, that you were in the ascendency, but I have to remind you of an old Welsh saying: don't count your fucking chickens before they are hatched, look you Boyo." I think this subtlety was lost on him, or perhaps it was lost on me.

What consummate joy I felt. OK, he was the architect of his own disaster, but, so what, I had one and a half points from two games and had beaten the second favourite. More than that, I knew it had hurt him big time.

The afternoon game was far less eventful and, following 40 moves of neither of us going anywhere, the man from Ghent agreed to an honourable draw. Were anyone present to doubt my credentials, I had, in three games, established my bona fides, albeit with a helping hand from god knows who.

Suddenly, I was the centre of attention from players and tournament officials alike, which I did not want, and had to make a hasty retreat to the nearby coffee house, knowing I would find my partner in crime there.

"Well, well, Dai, you never fail to amaze me."

"Ta, Vikram, you know as well as I do that my win over the German was a complete fluke, but who cares?"

"Being the sentient being I am, I would prefer to call it destiny or Kismet as we say in India. Whatever, it strengthens your cover just as long as you do not attract even more adulation from the travelling groupies by becoming the favourite to win. From now on it has to be softly-softly catchy monkey. Intelligence suggests your meet this evening is well timed."

"Fair enough my friend, I couldn't agree more. I am hoping to place said 'monkey' in a metaphorical cage for onward transmission to London starting tomorrow or Thursday at the very latest. I shall need you and any assists you have at your disposal to watch my back so attentively that anything that moves from my room towards room 741 before and from 8pm onwards, with the slightest hint of mal-intent, to be diverted or, at the very least, be made known to me in time for me to take evasive action. Understood?"

'Of course, Dai, fully understood. No leather goods and the guns that go with them will darken your doorstep."

I went to my room, spent an hour rehearsing my lines and then called room service for a light meal to be brought to me by 7pm – the last thing I wanted was to take a communal dinner in the main restaurant. I did, however, telephone Karim in his room to confirm our meeting was still on, which he did with alarming alacrity.

I deliberately delayed my arrival at Karim's door by ten minutes, just long enough to make him think I was not coming, but not long enough for him to start making unwanted telephone calls. The west wing of the seventh floor corridor seemed devoid of human presence as I made my way to room 741. I gently knocked on the door, which was opened by Karim rather too quickly.

"Come in, come in my friend. There have been developments."

He had the appearance of a man most troubled.

"Karim, is there a problem? You seem a little agitated?"

"David, I need to talk to you about why you are here in Tehran. My information, and please do not ask me how I know, tells me that there is an imperialist spy among the chess players who has instructions to take me to his country. And you are the only one who has been speaking with me. Is that the case, I have to know? Before you answer, I assume you know that I have an important position in my country's nuclear energy programme. In fact, I am the most important element in that process. I have a wife and two children, not to mention many close relatives in Iran, and so it is imperative that I don't put my or their lives at risk."

My mind was racing faster than a Formula 1 driver on speed. This was not how I had planned the evening would pan out. My first thought was how likely, if he has been tipped off by his state security, it was that my cover has been completely blown and what the fuck was I doing in a hotel room with no obvious escape route in downtown Tehran with a man of huge importance to the regime that owned him? And why, for heaven's sake had Vikram not anticipated this unwelcome turn of events?

" Karim, I am not at all sure what you are talking about. Unless I am mistaken, you invited me to your room to play some chess and not to engage in a world of fantasy. Also, I need to know why you think I am someone whom I am not and what has caused you to think that."

"Apologies, David, after we spoke yesterday I was called to the Ministry of Intelligence and interrogated about my conversations with you. I told them I had no idea what they were talking about and that I was affronted that they would even ask. They said that they had intelligence that suggested you might be a British spy sent to seduce me into defecting to the west.

You can imagine how I felt. I told them that I did not believe them, that I had taken the initiative and arranged to see you sociably tomorrow night rather than tonight and that I would do whatever they wanted me to do".

"Karim, you did well, very well indeed. The intelligence is correct. I am that spy and I do want to take you to the UK. The question is: do you want me to succeed or fail? If the latter, I might as well leave your room with a begging bowl and a white flag on a stick; if the former, and assuming they believed you about the timing of our meeting, we need to move very quickly. Like now. Whatever, this room is no longer safe, neither is mine. Do you wish to defect or not? My call would take too long to spell out in our current circumstances, but, essentially, if you wish to start a new life in the UK, I am the man who can facilitate it."

At that precise moment, there was a knock on the door. Fuck!! Karim looked at me with imploring eyes asking if our conversation had been monitored. I took a deep breath and, after covering the peep-hole with my wallet in case someone the other side of the door wanted to shoot me through the eye, I quietly opened the door.

Standing in front of me was a man dressed in hotel regalia carrying a tray covered by a white cloth.

"Room service, sir."

Vikram handed me the tray and his eyes darted right. Mine followed them but saw nothing of interest.

"Thank you. Wait I'll tip you in a second."

I found a few coins and pressed them into Vikram's hand, hopefully with a quizzical look on my face that said "What the hell is happening and what do I do next?".

"Have a good night, sir, and thank you very much".

With that he turned on his heels and disappeared stage left. I removed the cloth from the tray and, to my astonishment, found myself looking at a half-full syringe and an accompanying note.

By now Karim was in a semi-foetal position on the floor chanting what I took to be an Islamic prayer.

"Karim, it has now gone too far to turn back. I am now going to make a call that will hopefully trigger assistance and a way out of here."

My London briefing gave me the option of pressing one of three buttons on my secure phone. The first was to announce that I had turned my target, but that there was no immediate urgency attached to the exit arrangements; the second upped the anti somewhat and signalled that procedures had to be in place within 12 hours; and the third declared an emergency situation that demanded action within half an hour, maximum. I pressed the third button and said a prayer of my own.

The note advised me that the syringe contained enough drugs to knock out Karim for at least 3 hours and that I should await further developments, which would not take long.

I did my best to explain to Karim what was developing around us and convinced him to accept the injection, which he reluctantly did. Before doing so, however, he produced a briefcase, which he said contained papers of interest to my government. Without elaborating further, he insisted they should remain in my possession unless circumstances made their onward transmission essential and only then if his family's safety was vouchsafed. He made me promise on my honour and the lives of everyone dear to me that I would adhere to his wishes. I agreed to his terms and then administered the sedative. Within minutes, there was another knock on the door, this time by two (apparent) paramedics, in uniform and carrying a stretcher. Karim had gone to sleep on the carpet, was swiftly placed on the stretcher and, in no time at all, was being carried down the corridor towards the lift. Only, the crew ignored the lift and made for the emergency stairs, which they adroitly descended without missing a step, with me and no luggage, except the briefcase, in close attendance. I had left my passport and fingerprints at the hotel, not to mention a very good bottle of single malt. Such is life.

A fire door was more or less kicked open, and all four of us found ourselves in what looked like a loading bay. Whilst my eyes were adjusting to the darkness a set of headlights lit up the scene revealing an ambulance, which took but a few seconds to accommodate us and which was driven out of the compound at break-neck speed with siren wailing and lights flashing.

I assumed a lookout position and noticed two black sedans following us in quick succession. The ambulance jumped two or three sets of red lights, as they do, and, just beyond a busy inter-section screeched into a dimly lit side road some five or six seconds ahead of the pursuit teams, almost certainly MOI goons. Seamlessly, another ambulance roared into life and joined the main flow of traffic with equal noise and intensity. I noted that it had exactly the same registration plate as ours and correctly assumed it was there to attract the attention of our pursuers, which, thankfully, it duly did. "Neat", I thought.

CHAPTER 23

Karim and I were then transferred into a third vehicle, one that was specially chosen not to attract attention to itself, and were driven out of the city for an hour or so, mainly along country roads carrying very little traffic. Karim remained unconscious and therefore unconcerned (as yet).

The driver of the car was a Brit, who introduced himself as a 'friend' and colleague, but without revealing his name, not even a false one.

In clipped tones, he said: "Well done. You certainly cut the mustard. As you know, the escape plan will take you and your target into Turkey by helicopter, from where you will both be transferred to an RAF plane that will take you to a military base in southern England. Happy?"

"Ecstatic", I replied with no great enthusiasm.

The helicopter took off from a deserted field and flew low, to avoid radar detection, over Turkey's eastern border with Iran, presumably with the former's consent, and landed at a military site just inside the country's eastern border with Iran.

My immigration intelligence work had taken me to Turkey many times in recent years, during which I had been ably supported by British diplomats in Ankara, Istanbul and Izmir and had fostered excellent relationships with the Turkish Ministry of Interior, the Turkish National Police (TNP) as well as the Coast Guard, Customs and the Gendarmerie. Not that this counted for anything in my present circumstances, but it may have been, perhaps, one of the reasons why the Turkish authorities had agreed to the 'arrangement'. I shall never know, but I suspect it was far more to do with Turkey's wish to arrest Iran's aspirations to become a nuclear state.

The transfer was clinically quick, and, as we took off, Karim gradually and uncomfortably regained consciousness. His eyes opened and his mind began to clear, and worse, remember.

"Where are we, David? My head hurts like hell and I have only the slightest recollection of what happened before I passed out. Wait a minute, oh dear, yes I now remember..... my hotel room, the knocks on the door, the syringe, the blackness, the hopelessness of my life and those of my nearest and dearest. In the name of Allah, what have I done? Please tell me it is a bad dream."

"Afraid not, Old Boy. Your memory serves you well, and I have to tell you that our escape from Iran was a touch and go affair."

"You mean that we are not in my country, that we are somewhere else?"

"In one, Karim, we are on an RAF plane taking us to England, where we shall arrive in about three hours. I shall explain more when you are fully rested and more able to assimilate the information. For now, go back to sleep and dream of a happy life for you and your family in a country that is more suited to your needs, talents and creativity. But your chess, by the way, is crap." He smiled weakly and needed no more encouragement to follow my advice.

Job done or should I say, last job done. Even a rigged Lottery win would not entice me to get involved in a fourth mission. My nerves were torn to shreds, I was drinking hazardously (Rhiannon would laugh until she peed herself, adding 'since when?') and I was two years off retirement. Let's get Karim to where he wants to be, In'shallah, and me to a place I feel comfortable in with people who liked me or disliked me for who I was.

The plane landed at Brize Norton in Oxfordshire, where the chief immigration officer in charge of immigration controls was known to me, was met by a small party of three, presumably SIS, and disgorged its human cargo onto a wet, but hugely welcome tarmac. Karim, a bit weak in the knees, was helped to a waiting vehicle, whilst I was taken to one side by an amiable SIS officer, who assured me everything was right with the world and would I like a lift to London.

"What will happen to the poor bastard?" I asked.

"Nothing worse than would have happened had he remained in Tehran, I can assure you. Don't worry, he and his immediate family will be well taken care of. From what I know, which isn't very much, he is now part of the Crown jewels – a treasure to be protected for all time."

"Can you please pass on to Justin Smith, if that's his real name, that I would like to talk with Karim before he disappears into a protection progamme?"

"Of course I will. My feeling, though, is that Justin will be your welcoming party when we reach London."

By the time we arrived in London it was after midnight. My escort dropped me off outside the cream and white edifice known as 'the MI6 Building', original or what?, otherwise referred to as Lego Land or Babylon-on Thames. I was met at the main door and taken to Justin's office.

"Dai, what can I say? You did everything we asked of you, nay far more, and I, the Service, and the country, are hugely indebted to you for your bravery, success, inventiveness and, I have to say, brilliant chess play."

He pushed towards me a tumbler of very good scotch and held out a congratulatory hand, which I shook without any real feeling of accomplishment. Why I knew not. The whisky went down at a rate of knots and was quickly replenished. Justin was looking tired and drawn and after a few more welcoming words said: "We are all a little fatigued, you most of all, so can I suggest we both get some sleep on the premises and meet in the morning for a debrief session?"

I was past caring and nodded my assent, at the same time grabbing the bottle of the 18 year old bottle of Macallam, sherry oak Speyside, I noted, which accompanied me to bed and temporary oblivion. Before parting company, however, I looked Justin squarely in the eyes and said: "If Karim's family are not properly taken care of I shall be most upset, probably to the point of blowing a very loud whistle, if you follow my drift."

"All taken care of, believe me my friend."

I resisted my usual barbed repost and just limply nodded my acknowledgement of what I knew to be a commitment of statement rather than of faith. A couple more amber nectars and I was well and truly away with the fairies, my last thought being: "shit, I forgot to ring Rhiannon!"

I was woken with a strong cup of good quality coffee, a towel for my shower and a change of underwear. This preceded a full English breakfast and an escort to a conference room, in which were seated six people, including Justin, all bright eyed and bushy tailed. I scanned the room for another familiar face, but saw none. I sat down next to a worried looking Justin and waited for someone to make the next move.

It came from an imposing man whom I took to be the head honcho.

"Mr Morgan, my name is Simon Hunter, Chairman of the Joint Intelligence Committee, which is part of the Cabinet Office and responsible for providing ministers and senior officials with co-ordinated, inter-departmental intelligence assessments on a range of issues of immediate and longer term importance to national security, primarily in the fields of security, defence and foreign affairs. I apologise if that seems like a mouthful, especially as I know from your intel role within the Home Office that you are more than aware of who we are and what we do.

I also apologise for fielding such a large team to probe your very difficult time in Iran, for which I and my colleagues are exceedingly indebted. I know how fatigued you must feel and how much you yearn to rejoin your family, but, please, bear with us whilst we clear our lines and try to understand all you have experienced in what must have been a most dangerous and challenging mission."

"Not at all, sir. I am at your disposal and quite ready to display my wares and tears."

"Excellent, I would have expected no less. Can we start with the your first meeting with your target, Karim? It would seem, from the reports I have read, that he was quite happy to meet with you on a one-to-one basis and with, can I say rather vulgarly, no real foreplay. For a man in such an exalted position in a country fraught with intrigue and danger, this might be interpreted as excessive risk, don't you think?"

" Sir Simon, I am indeed aware of the function of JIC and the role you play in it as its Chair. Yes, I was surprised at the speed of the invitation, but I rationalised it on the basis of intelligence received from my Indian friends rather than the SIS." I sensed an uneasy shifting of position by Justin, but carried on regardless.

"It would have been helpful to me to have been told by my parent department that Karim is a practising homosexual, albeit of the AC/DC variety, which I think accounts for the boldness of his approach."

Sir Simon fleetingly looked at Justin with a raised eyebrow then returned to the fray.

"That's all very interesting, and a lead that I'm sure Justin will wish to take forward. My next question is why Karim's minders, at no point whilst you were in his hotel room, came to his 'rescue', given the proximity of their surveillance and the importance of their charge?"

"I really don't know the answer to that one. I can only assume that SIS' Indian agent played a hand in it - he certainly was there for me on the night.

"Before we go any further, can I ask if you think that Karim's defection was pre-planned by his country's security service and that he is now here as a double-agent?"

"I am 100 percent sure that this is not the case. I had the opportunity of watching Karim go through the turmoil of 'should I, shouldn't I', and am convinced that he had not thought it through. He knew what he didn't want to happen and he hoped that what he aspired to would be the answer to all his prayers.

Please, do not go down the road of double-agent. That he is not. If his family can be brought to the UK to join him, you will have a friend for life. Of that I am sure."

A question followed from one of the 'team', who decided to remain anonymous.

"Did Karim make an approach to you of a sexual nature?"

"Not at all, but I was in his room only for a short time before things started to kick-off. If this was his intention he was not in a hurry to declare it".

A second voice and question.

"Why, might I ask, do you wish to see Karim again? A little unusual in your game wouldn't you say?"

"My game is, or, at least, was chess. The 007 bit is very much a side interest and one that I now formally resign from. Justin, please note. The reason I want to speak with Karim is simply to assure him that he has made the right decision and to wish him and his family a happy and rewarding time in the UK."

"How do you assess the worth of Karim now that he might be damaged good?"

"Sorry, I think that is a no-brainer question. Someone else in the world of British security will have to evaluate that one. He will only be 'damaged goods' if you lot deem it so. My advice to all of you is to treat him with the kid gloves he deserves. Then, and only then, might you get a proper return on your investment.

Sir Simon resumed pole position.

"Quite, and I see no reason for your request to see Karim once more to be refused. Justin will make the arrangements, but I would caution you, David, not to reveal too much about your personal circumstances. Just in case......Well, I think that is enough for one day. May I take the opportunity of once again thanking you for bringing a most difficult mission to a successful conclusion. Your efforts were well crafted, well delivered and extremely well received. Oh, by the by, would you have won that tournament had you stayed to the end?"

"Thank you for your kind words. As to the chess question, not a bloody chance!"

With that Justin rose from his chair and escorted me to his room.

CHAPTER 24

Justin was not a happy bunny, a happy bunny he was not.

"Thanks, Dai, you really dropped me in it in there. If we'd known about the target's sexual proclivities we would have told you, but all the evidence pointed to a happily married boffin who was straight down the middle."

"Depends which 'middle' you're talking about, Justin. The fact is that the IB's intelligence on Karim was better than yours. Doesn't that worry you a tad? Whilst the omission would, in all probability, not have proved fatal to the operation, it was a major piece of intelligence and was, as such, very important for me to know about, don't you think?"

"I agree and will rerun the intelligence trail - reports, logs and the rest of it - to try and find out how it was overlooked. As to meeting Karim, I can arrange for you to do so next week, if this is convenient to you. We need a full week to debrief him and to place him in a permanent safe house with his family, whom I expect to arrive tomorrow. As we speak they are out of Iran and awaiting onward transportation to the UK. I would just reiterate what Sir Simon Hunter said about not getting too lovey-dovey with our man. Even if, as I'm sure is the case, he is legit, circumstances change and you should not expose yourself to reprisals from a country that is currently spitting feathers. We're waiting the first salvo from the Iranian ambassador any time now and along the lines: 'We have reason to believe that the British government has kidnapped one of our top scientists, which imperialist action runs contrary to national and international law. We demand his immediate return, or else'. It's the 'or else' that worries me."

I spent the next several hours writing my report, having firstly telephoned a frantic Rhiannon, who was beside herself with worry and not a little angry. "No cuddles tonight then?" I ventured to ask.

Leaving the cream and green building, I took myself to a nearby Spanish bar-restaurant, which I had frequented several times before with some good friends. I ordered a large Spanish lager and a few of my favourite tapas, all of which I devoured with huge enjoyment. This gave me some quality time to reflect on the last few days, which, in retrospect, had been unusual and challenging, even in my topsy-turvy life.

An ex Immigration Service, now SIS friend if mine arrived unannounced on the scene, sat down at my table and said:

"Dai, mine's a pint, not that I drink on duty."

Two hours later, we're both half pissed and fondly remembering days of Yore, which, I have to say, were far more effective, honest and transparent than the ones I found myself in now.

I then made my way to Victoria station and onward to my west Sussex home and family.

Despite this happy interlude, I knew in my heart that things had come to a pretty pass. No more could I fool myself that I was something special. My bones felt very old and tired, and all I yearned for was a simple, quiet career denouement that would take me into the sunset of my retirement.

I must have looked half dead when I walked into the house, because Rhiannon, normally quick of temper and tongue, said:

"Welcome home, Dai my love. You look like a sack of shit, so you are either drunk or ill, or both."

"Hi my ever-loving, you can't say 'either' for more than one alternative, though I have to say that they all apply to my present condition. No chance of an early night, I suppose?"

"Dai, sit down, have something to eat and discuss your other options after you give me my present, not that your chances are as optimistic as you might wish. And can I say something that I know will annoy you intensely? Don't answer that, I'm going to ask you anyway. I'm not sure what has been going on in your other life for the last thirty plus years, but don't think I don't know that you have been up to something I would not like. That's a given. I am more concerned about your state of mind, which is bordering on implosion.

Could we talking about another woman in your life, 'cos, if that's so we've got a serious problem? I've suspected for a long time that you have been seeing someone behind my back, I can almost smell her on you sometimes. Is it someone from your office? As you know, I am that straightforward, naive sole who believes most things I am told, but now, I'm not so sure. For heaven's sake, Dai, let's put this to rest before it destroys both of us."

I knew that I had to say something to bring her peace of mind, but I was not sure how to phrase it without compromising my alter ego.

"Rhiannon, you could not be further from the truth. 'Yes', my mind is a bit frazzled at the moment, but that is only a temporary thing. 'No', I am not having an affair, but you should know that I have work-related difficulties, which are nothing to do with my Immigration Service role. You will have to trust me on this one, my love. One day I might be able to explain the missing bits, but not yet. OK?"

" OK Dai. No more questions for now. Eat up and tell me what you have been doing, not that I'll believe a word of it."

I had not realised how much Rhiannon was jealous of the gaps in our relationship, and, let's face it, they were many and not at all easily explained.

"Dai, I said eat your supper and give me my present!"

The banter was helpful, but barely covered the cracks. Rhiannon knew there was something wrong, I knew there was something wrong and, if Rupert Murdoch knew there was something wrong, everyone else in the world would know there was something wrong. I felt physically and emotionally drained, and wished only to give my wife a cwtch – look it up if you are that interested - and to immerse myself in 'how to enjoy your retirement' handbooks.

I think Rhiannon could have given me a far harder time had she put her mind to it. There was a lot of built-up resentment, if truth were known, but there was also a genuine affection on both sides of the relationship, one that had been nurtured over a long period of time. But let's not get too sentimental: there were some hard times ahead and I had to steel myself to them.

The following week I received a call on the secure line in my office from Justin, who told me that I could see Karim that day and no later. Apologies for the late notice, but that was how it was. Yes or no?

I said I would be there and asked for directions, which I memorised. I took a train from my Sussex station to Victoria and a black cab to my destination in North London. The safe house was, as it was supposed to be, ordinary and unremarkable. The day was wet and windy, and I did not have a good feel for our reunion. Don't ask me why, I just didn't.

I pressed the doorbell and waited. The voice on the intercom said: "Who is it?". I replied: "Dai for Karim." "Just a minute." The door was opened by a large man, who was confident in his ability to kick the shit out of you if you were the wrong person on his tick-box card.

" Hi", I said, " I'm Dai, you should be expecting me."

There followed a grunt and a nod, which I took to be an invitation to enter. The big man then proceeded to frisk me for weaponry and, having satisfied himself, grudgingly I thought, that I was clean, took me to an empty room. Within minutes a door opened and Karim appeared, looking tired and withdrawn.

"Karim, my friend, how are you?"

"David, I am very pleased to see you again. I'm fine and my immediate family are here with me. Which is good." Looking sideways at the minder, Karim said:

"I need to speak with you on a one-to-one basis, if you know what I mean".

"Sure", I replied, "I couldn't agree more."

The minder threw me a glance, which attracted a nod from me, and he duly retreated to another room. I was acutely aware that the whole house was wired for sound, and probably more, and that I would have to be circumspect in what I said to Karim and to try and guide him down the same road.

"Karim, I wanted to see you again before parting company, possibly forever. Before you say anything, be aware that the walls have ears, if not eyes, which is to say that I only want you to be truthful and straightforward in everything you say. Understood?"

Karim espied the room through different eyes, focused on mine and said:

"David, firstly, I am indebted to you for all you have done for me and my family. Without your help I would still be in a state of turmoil with no hope of redemption. You have given us a chance of a new life in a new country, for which I cannot thank you enough. Before you leave, you must meet my wife and children, who are equally grateful for all you have done."

"That would be nice, Karim, but before doing so, perhaps you could answer one or two questions? The first is to do with our meeting in Tehran. You will have worked out that I initially made the running, but what I am less sure about is why you took the bait so quickly. It seemed to me that you were too quick to invite me to your hotel room with only the briefest of contact. Let me say before you reply that I was already aware of your, shall we say, attraction to male friends and all that entails - a leaning I took full advantage of in the build-up to our relationship".

Karim looked at me with doleful eyes and said:

"David, I did indeed feel attracted to you, but it may come as a surprise that this was based mainly on a feeling that you were someone I could relate to on an emotional, rather than a physical level. You are a top chess player, of that I am sure, but, more than that, you possess excellent people skills, which was something I needed then and I need now."

"You also know, Karim, that my masters will take full advantage of your scientific brilliance, of which you will be doubtless fully aware. That's part of the deal, I'm afraid. Please do yourself a favour and comply unreservedly with their every demand. That way you will find yourself closer to your dream for a better life."

"Thank you, David, for your kind words of wisdom. I just hope that your colleagues treat me with the same touch and sensitivity. Please, come and meet my family, but before doing so, can you assure me that the papers I gave to you in Tehran remain in your safe keeping?" "Of course, Karim, I gave you my word."

I left the safe house with mixed feelings of hope and angst. I was not at all sure how Karim would react to the pressures of exile and disconnection with his home country. My professional instincts told me that I had done as much as I could to bring the mission to a successful conclusion. Nothing, however, prepared me for the news of his subsequent suicide that followed the sad fate of his close family members in Iran. I learned of this just before my retirement in 2006 and spent the next twelve months in sackcloth and ashes, for which read deep depression. What an eye-watering waste of a lovely human being!

CHAPTER 25

The last twelve months of my working life were, by and large, otherwise uneventful. I caught up with my day job and started to think who would succeed me as the intelligence manager of my excellent team. I now understand that those in charge have relabelled everything, including the nomenclature of the Immigration Service, to give the impression that nothing of note preceded it. Embarrassingly, I recently was told of a high level note referring to the (possible) issue of a British Identity Card, which included reference to 'The UK **Boarder** Agency (UKBA)'. Apart from an inability to spell something that should not have replaced the words 'UK Immigration Service', what a silly gaffe to make. It would be less worrying were this to be an isolated local problem. But, no, it is a systemic, greasy pole, self-advancement process that pervades the Home Office (and, indeed, the most of the Civil Service) and one that will not get any better until the powers that be and their lack-lustre progeny have been replaced by the twin pillars of leadership and achievement, which are no longer predicated on a foundation of intelligence, experience, knowledge, loyalty and nous; rather, they are represented by spin, change for change sake, self-advancement and sheer, fucking stupidity.

Over the years I have seen the so called 'Great and the Good' come and go with no real or worthwhile change to the landscape. Now they are younger (let's not get into the gender split) and stupider, mostly with no in depth knowledge of what was once held to be a governmental beacon of excellence. You, the reader, might think I am a silly old fart, who, frustratingly did not make it to the highest ranks. You could not be further from the truth.

Au contraire, I enjoyed most of my career in the Immigration Service, to which I believe I contributed a good deal in terms of innovative thought, sound management and landmark deliveries. Not many of my more recent senior managers can say the same.

I am aware that most, but not all, of the backbone of my erstwhile colleagues can't wait to retire, preferably with a package. I am also aware of the strength of the 'old guard', some of who annually foregather at a pub in Waterloo on the first Wednesday in November to celebrate the rail journey from the Cape to Cairo and the fact they are still alive and able to remember the old times. Were they better? Of course they were. Were they more productive? Of course they were.

Before I fall off my soapbox with my hubris firmly shoved up my nether region, I shall return to the main story? I have now reached the age of 62. I could bore you to death with the list of my bodily ailments; I drink too much; and I have the memory of a retard. Why, then, would anyone of sane mind ask me, once again, to do something for the national good that completely transcended my ability to do it? This is, of course, a rhetorical question, given my past performances.

The approach came out of the blue. Rhiannon was still working, hating every minute of it, and I busied myself as a househusband – and not a bad one at that if I say so myself. I did the shopping, a bit of cleaning, a few jobs around the house and garden, but mostly I did the cooking. Not a day passed when I did not plug into UK TV

Food programmes. I learned how to cook a plethora of British and foreign meals, some better than others, but always done from the heart. Rhiannon never lost an opportunity to list my mistakes, but I knew this was nothing but blatant jealousy.

What on earth did they, could they want from me now?!

CHAPTER 26

I find myself sat in a chair looking at a slightly broader based Justin, who, judging by the size of his present office, has had one or two more lifts up that slippery ladder.

"Dai, good to see you and thanks for making the journey to the Metropolis. It must have come as a huge surprise to you to get my call, particularly as you had made it all too clear that the last job was your last job. Before I elaborate, can I offer you some refreshment. A glass of something I know you like, perhaps?"

Why did he look so pompously pleased with himself when revealing a titbit of acquired knowledge?

"Justin, thank you 'no', the only reason I made the journey to Vauxhall Cross was that I could not believe that you were making a serious approach. For God's sake man, I have one foot in the grave, am about as agile as an octogenarian endomorph in a wheel chair and find it difficult to remember what day it. How on earth can I be of further use to the SIS?"

"You know about the sad demise of Karim, dreadful business that it was. But his wife and children are still here and, for some reason, trust nobody in the organisation except you, which is a bit rich given you were the one who brought him out."

I couldn't make up my mind whether to chin him or just remove myself from his presence. Instead, I gave him the best withering look I could muster and said:

"Justin, get to the point as quickly as you can, 'cos otherwise I'm out of here in less time than it takes to get shit off a shovel".

"I apologise if I have offended you – my wife is always telling me to think before I speak – so I shall cut to the chase more in hope than expectation that you will take up the challenge.

Karim's widow, Aisha, is threatening to tell all, a situation we would wish to avoid and to which you should also feel opposed. VEVAK would like nothing better than to visit sunny Sussex, I'm sure."

I noted the attempt at a chess move, which was as subtle as a custard pie in the face.

"I see all too clearly where you are coming from, Justin. You want me to speak with Aisha and convince her that her future lies in the UK; that any indiscretion on her part could, nay would result in her and the children being returned to Iran so that she could, whilst she still could, tend the graves of her dead relatives. Yes?"

"As usual, Dai, you see through my game plan, and your reading of the situation is entirely correct. What say you, Old Boy?. We would, of course, provide a cast iron back-up team and put at your disposal anything, within reason, you needed to accomplish the task."

I sat there for what seemed an eternity, but was no nearer coming to a decision than I was when the mission was first tabled. If I declined the invitation, I could walk away and wait for the enemy without to come within, or I could grasp the nettle and do what I knew I would do. Not for MI6, but for Aisha and Karim.

"Justin, despite your clumsy attempt at enticement, I shall do your dirty work, provided you agree to certain demands.

In order, they are:

1. I call the shots when they matter, like all of the time unless I say otherwise;
2. I am consulted before any nastiness takes place;
3. and I am informed of all – and I mean **all** - moves, real or imagined, from the enemy.

Agreed?"

"Dai, unreservedly agreed. When can you make the visit to the safe house?"

"No time like the present. Please contact Aisha to see if now is convenient to her and, if so, let me have the current address."

Justin did as was bid and, within minutes, had furnished me with the address, which was also in north London. I took the usual tradecraft travelling precautions (several modes of transport, back-tracking and property surveillance) and, only when I was satisfied there were no unwelcome followers or observers, did I ring the doorbell.

Aisha opened the door very slowly. She looked drawn and pale and her eyes bore the signs of great sadness.

"Come in, please, Mr Morgan". My heart sank as I walked into the apartment. The children were at school and would be for another 2 hours, which was more than sufficient for my purposes.

"May I call you Aisha? Although we have briefly met once before, I feel I know you quite well from my talks with Karim, whose tragic death has saddened me greatly."

"Yes, of course. Karim spoke very fondly of you, so much so that I was prepared to speak with no-one else on the subject of my future intentions, of which I assume you have been told."

"Yes, Aisha, I have been told. And you must call me Dai, which is my nickname. I feel desperately guilty about what has happened to your life since you and Karim came to England. I tried my best to arrange for his relatives in Iran to be protected and, preferably, brought to the UK. That this did not happen is a source of huge regret to me, and, quite honestly, I have no excuse to offer you."

"Thank you for that, Dai. Karim was a very sensitive man and found himself in a very difficult position, both in his job and, to be perfectly frank, in his intimate preferences. I'm sure I don't have to say more other than to tell you that he hated being largely responsible for our country's nuclear policy".

The conversation meandered around this double statement of fact, my mind desperately searching for the right words to console her and to bring about a change of mind. I decided that the children offered the best prospect, and I played on this shamelessly.

"Aisha, I do not blame you for wanting to expose the British government for a situation not of your making. As you have said, Karim was not happy in his work and was more than ready to accept a way out. He was, indeed, an intelligent and sensitive man, who will be sorely missed by you and the children.

On the subject of the children, I am authorised to tell you that they will continue to enjoy private education throughout the whole of their primary and secondary schooling and that you will receive a generous stipendiary and free accommodation for the whole of your life in the UK. It will come as no surprise to you to learn that this offer requires your complete silence and total discretion as to the circumstances that led to Karim's decision to leave Iran".

Aisha's eyes betrayed her, and I knew I had begun to influence her to go in the direction I wanted. But nothing is certain in the world of espionage, unlike death and taxes in the real world.

"Were I to agree to your terms, would your service also agree to bring my parents and siblings and their families to the UK and to provide them with the same protection and financial support?"

'Nice one, Aisha', I thought – an excellent chess move that demanded a very good reply.

"My masters anticipated this request and briefed me on how to respond to it. Your immediate family in Iran is large and have not experienced any reprisals thus far. That is not to underestimate their vulnerability. To bring them here under a protection programme would be a logistical nightmare and would make it far more difficult to guarantee your and your children's safety. Far better, they think, to relocate them in a conducive part of neighbouring Iraq, which is becoming increasingly stable and in which they would enjoy a similar life-style among their own religious sect, aided by an acceptable level of financial assistance from HMG. I might add, without wishing to give you the impression of unfair pressure, that a full confession would by no means safeguard you, your children and your family members from the more extreme elements of your government. What do you say?" A long wait.

"Let me think about it. I promise a response by next week at the latest if you agree to act for me and keep me fully informed as to developments in respect of my family's wellbeing should they and I agree to your government's terms."

I felt I had gone as far as I could for now and therefore agreed to her conditions and left. She knew that she could not contact me directly, which was what she wanted, and that she would have to do so via a secure telephone at Vauxhall Cross, to where I returned for a debriefing by Justin. I also harboured a feeling of doubt that she was being totally candid with me, but I decided to let the feeling incubate whilst I prepared myself for a bit of Justin bating.

"Hi Dai, sorry if that sounds like a South Korean car, but I couldn't resist it. How was the lovely Aisha and how did she respond to what I think is a very generous offer?"

"Hi Justin-case you've got another half-arsed joke to get out of your system. My mission went as well as I think it could have, all things being equal, which, of course, they never are. The lady will consider her options and get back to us within a week with her answer. I have, however, one or two nagging doubts. Why, for example, has she put all her trust in a man she hardly knows and who has been instrumental in her late husband's death? OK, Karim may have told her I could be trusted to play fair. But so what? She and her two children are alone in a foreign country, which promised only financial reward for her loss and some sort of relocation programme for her nearest and dearest in Iran.

There's more to this than meets the eye. Perhaps the MOI have already put the squeeze on her – a bit surprising her family have not met with the same fate as Karim's, don't you think? Can you put her under maximum surveillance over the next several days and I mean maximum. I think she has already been got-at and that somebody else is pulling the strings."

"Interesting take on the case, I have to say, Dai. Let's see what she's up to, shall we? It wouldn't be the first time the Service has been targeted by the so-called innocent party, and, I'm sure, not the last."

I returned home a troubled man.

CHAPTER 27

My mobile went off 5 days' later, alerting me by codeword to use my secure phone. This I did with great speed and not a little foreboding.

"Dai, bad news, I'm afraid. Your qualms were fully justified. Not only is the lady fully in the power of the MOI, she is one of their top operatives. Her marriage to Karim was State arranged, as were her two pregnancies. She knows about Karim's homosexual tendencies, as I think she told you, and she was there to ensure he otherwise stayed on the straight and narrow. I think we can be sure he did not tell Aisha of his decision to come here or else the exit would have been terminated long before your dash for freedom got off the ground.

Within two hours of your departure from her apartment, she had a visit from a person well known to us at the Iranian embassy. I'm surprised it took that long, given the importance of your meeting. Perhaps she was, after all, considering her options?"

'Hmm. Not good, eh? What to do with the damaged goods?"

"Get your arse up to the factory as quick as you can. We have a high-level emergency conference at 1500hrs today."

My journey to London was spent trying to figure out the possible moves and counter-moves. On the one hand we had a captive audience who was apparently unaware that she, and her handlers, had been tumbled; on the other hand we had to concede that the Iranians had proof positive that UK PLC had been up to no good on the ancient stage of political espionage. Horns of dilemma or what? What I did not know was what Karim had divulged to his British quizzers. Had he told them the full extent of his involvement in Iran's nuclear proliferation? If not, the cards were not necessarily stacked against us.

I reached the green and cream at 1415hrs and, after my brief case was searched and found only to hold some papers, mostly in hieroglyphics, was escorted, with just one short-term diversion, to Justin's office at 1445hrs on the dot. He was clearly in an agitated state of mind and kept looking at his watch to ensure we did not miss the meeting.

"Dai, I have to tell you that we have a mega problem on our hands. We are about to face the Joint Intelligence Committee with Sir Simon looking none too pleased. Our poker hand is based more on style rather than substance and we could be blown away if we don't get the JIC's backing."

" Justin, just one question. Did Karim spill the beans before he met his maker?"

'Good question, as usual Dai, the truth of the matter is that I do not know. You might ask why I don't know, but the fact remains I don't."

A short walk back to the same conference room I had been interrogated in by the JIC not long ago found Justin and I sat opposite a bevy of dour-faced inquisitors, whose sole purpose in life seemed to be to make our lives as miserable as possible.

The normally affable Sir Simon Hunter looked tired and tense, and lost no time in opening the proceedings.

"Mr Morgan, the last time we met I had a good feeling about how this caper would unravel. Now I'm not so sure. I am told that we have been harbouring an enemy of the State, at some expense I have to say, and that she is now about the blow a very loud whistle, the sound of which could reverberate around the globe. How am I doing so far? Don't answer that.

I also know that the product from the target's protection is limited in so far as we know little more about Iran's nuclear activities than we did before we expatriated him. In short, we are up the fucking Khyber without a paddle. What do you have to say for yourself? You can answer that."

I could feel Justin's eyes boring into me, wondering if he would be putting his office possessions into a cardboard box at the close of play.

"Sir Simon, I know this must come as a shock to you and your committee. In my defence I had no control over the intelligence debriefing process, nor over the protection arrangements of Karim and his family".

"Sir, I am not asking you about your culpability. I am asking you what the fuck, and I make no excuse for my profane language, you were doing whilst London was burning?"

"Sir Simon, please don't shoot the messenger. All is not lost. Before Karim and I left Iran, he gave me a stack of top-secret papers that tracks every, and I mean every move Iran has made to join the nuclear club. He swore me to secrecy unless there was no alternative in revealing its content, lest his family suffer as a consequence. As of today these papers are now with the appropriate SIS research and development unit, here in this building, and should provide all you need to know about something Iran will not wish to make public now or forever."

There followed a stunned silence, which seemed to last for ever.

"Mr Morgan, are you telling us that we have a Royal flush to play should we get our hand called by the opposition? Are you telling us that, to mix my metaphors, your chess skills have outwitted the best that the MOI have to offer? If so, I, on behalf of the government and my committee, cannot thank you enough. Because of the promised quality of the product and because you had every reason to suppose Karim was delivering the goods in the debriefing process, I shall not ask you why you held on to the material for nearly two years or where you kept it. As an intelligence manager I assume you had the means to do so securely."

There followed a sitting ovation. The applause was almost deafening and Justin nearly fainted.

CHAPTER 28

All's well that ends well, as they say in the best children's books. The international incident did not happen; Iran's nuclear development was put on hold (for a while, at least); Aisha returned to her homeland with her children and her family remained there also; and I retired completely from my covert life and from my professional career and happily carried out my duties as a househusband and crap golfer. My farewell bash was well attended thanks to the tireless and imaginative organisational skills of my then colleague and always good friend, Phil Canning, whom Barack Obama would do well to recruit as his next campaign fund raiser.

Needless to say, there was no kneeling before QEII, nor was there a spectacular remuneration from my erstwhile employer of the night. It did not matter a toss. I was only too pleased to have resurrected my chess skills, albeit briefly, and to have beaten, albeit luckily, one of the best chess Masters in Europe.

Retirement also gave me the opportunity, house-husband lists aside, to sit down and write a novella, the contents of which are partly fictional, or should that be factional?

For a poor little chess boy, I also felt I had made up for blowing the junior British championship all those years ago because of a lack of 'bottle' and an insufficient desire to win.

Hey ho, Never Say Dai, eh?

THE END

Printed in the United Kingdom by
Lightning Source UK Ltd., Milton Keynes
138263UK00001B/40/P